This Is How
You Lose
the Time War

This Is How You Lose the Time War

AMAL EL-MOHTAR
&
MAX GLADSTONE

SAGA PRESS

LONDON SYDNEY **NEW YORK** TORONTO NEW DELHI

SAGA PRESS
AN IMPRINT OF SIMON & SCHUSTER, INC.

1230 AVENUE OF THE AMERICAS, NEW YORK, NEW YORK 10020

Text copyright © 2019 by Amal El-Mohtar and Max Gladstone
Cover photographs copyright © 2019 by iStock/PrinPrince (ultramarine flycatcher) and iStock/Saddako (northern cardinal)
For information about special discounts for bulk purchases, please contact Simon & Schuster Special Sales at 1-866-506-1949 or business@simonandschuster.com.
The Simon & Schuster Speakers Bureau can bring authors to your live event. For more information or to book an event, contact the Simon & Schuster Speakers Bureau at 1-866-248-3049 or visit our website at www.simonspeakers.com.
Cover design by Greg Stadnyk; interior design by Hilary Zarycky
The text for this book was set in New Caledonia.
Manufactured in the United States of America
First Saga Press trade paperback edition March 2020
23
The Library of Congress has cataloged the hardcover edition as follows:
Names: El-Mohtar, Amal, author. | Gladstone, Max, author.
Title: This is how you lose the time war / Amal El-Mohtar and Max Gladstone.
Description: First edition. | New York, NY : Saga Press, 2019.
Identifiers: LCCN 2018017464 | ISBN 9781534431003 (hardcover) | ISBN 9781534430990 (softcover) | ISBN 9781534431010 (eBook)
Subjects: LCSH: Time travel—Fiction. | GSAFD: Science fiction.
Classification: LCC PR9199.4.E424 T48 2019 | DDC 813/.6—dc23
LC record available at https://lccn.loc.gov/2018017464

To you.

PS. Yes, you.

This Is How
You Lose
the Time War

When Red wins, she stands alone.

Blood slicks her hair. She breathes out steam in the last night of this dying world.

That was fun, she thinks, but the thought sours in the framing. It was clean, at least. Climb up time's threads into the past and make sure no one survives this battle to muddle the futures her Agency's arranged—the futures in which her Agency rules, in which Red herself is possible. She's come to knot this strand of history and sear it until it melts.

She holds a corpse that was once a man, her hands gloved in its guts, her fingers clutching its alloy spine. She lets go, and the exoskeleton clatters against rock. Crude technology. Ancient. Bronze to depleted uranium. He never had a chance. That is the point of Red.

After a mission comes a grand and final silence. Her weapons and armor fold into her like roses at dusk. Once flaps of pseudoskin settle and heal and the programmable matter of her clothing knits back together, Red looks, again, something like a woman.

She paces the battlefield, seeking, making sure.

She has won, yes, she has won. She is certain she has won. Hasn't she?

Both armies lie dead. Two great empires broke themselves here, each a reef to the other's hull. That is what she came to do. From their ashes others will rise, more suited to her Agency's ends. And yet.

There was another on the field—no groundling like the time-moored corpses mounded by her path, but a real player. Someone from the other side.

Few of Red's fellow operatives would have sensed that opposing presence. Red knows only because Red is patient, solitary, careful. She studied for this engagement. She modeled it backward and forward in her mind. When ships were not where they were supposed to be, when escape pods that should have been fired did not, when certain fusillades came thirty seconds past their cue, she noticed.

Twice is coincidence. Three times is enemy action.

But why? Red has done what she came to do, she thinks. But wars are dense with causes and effects, calculations and strange attractors, and all the more so are wars in time. One spared life might be worth more to the other side than all the blood that stained Red's hands today. A fugitive becomes a queen or a scientist or, worse, a poet. Or her child does, or a smuggler she trades jackets with in some distant spaceport. And all this blood for nothing.

Killing gets easier with practice, in mechanics and technique. Having killed never does, for Red. Her fellow agents do not feel the same, or they hide it better.

It is not like Garden's players to meet Red on the same field at the same time. Shadows and sure things are more their style. But there is one who would. Red knows her, though they have never met. Each player has their signature. She recognizes patterns of audacity and risk.

Red may be mistaken. She rarely is.

Her enemy would relish such a magic trick: twisting to her own ends all Red's grand work of murder. But it's not enough to suspect. Red must find proof.

So she wanders the charnel field of victory and seeks the seeds of her defeat.

A tremor passes through the soil—do not call it earth. The planet dies. Crickets chirp. Crickets survive, for now, among the crashed ships and broken bodies on this crumbling plain. Silver moss devours steel, and violet flowers choke the dead guns. If the planet lasted long enough, the vines that sprout from the corpses' mouths would grow berries.

It won't, and neither will they.

On a span of blasted ground, she finds the letter.

It does not belong. Here there should be bodies mounded between the wrecks of ships that once sailed the stars. Here there should be the death and dirt and blood of a successful op. There should be moons disintegrating overhead, ships aflame in orbit.

There should not be a sheet of cream-colored paper, clean save a single line in a long, trailing hand: *Burn before reading.*

Red likes to feel. It is a fetish. Now she feels fear. And eagerness.

She was right.

She searches shadows for her hunter, her prey. She hears infrasonic, ultrasound. She thirsts for contact, for a new, more worthy battle, but she is alone with the corpses and the splinters and the letter her enemy left.

It is a trap, of course.

Vines curl through eye sockets, twine past shattered portholes. Rust flakes fall like snow. Metal creaks, stressed, and shatters.

It is a trap. Poison would be crude, but she smells none. Perhaps a noovirus in the message—to subvert her thoughts, to seed a trigger, or merely to taint Red with suspicion in her Commandant's eyes. Perhaps if she reads this letter, she will be recorded, exposed, blackmailed for use as a double agent. The enemy is insidious. Even if this is but the opening gambit of a longer game, by reading it Red risks Commandant's wrath if she is discovered, risks seeming a traitor be she never so loyal.

The smart and cautious play would be to leave. But the letter is a gauntlet thrown, and Red has to know.

She finds a lighter in a dead soldier's pocket. Flames catch in the depths of her eyes. Sparks rise, ashes fall, and letters form on the paper, in that same long, trailing hand.

Red's mouth twists: a sneer, a mask, a hunter's grin.

The letter burns her fingers as the signature takes shape. She lets its cinders fall.

Red leaves then, mission failed and accomplished at once, and climbs downthread toward home, to the braided future her Agency shapes and guards. No trace of her remains save cinders, ruins, and millions dead.

The planet waits for its end. Vines live, yes, and crickets, though no one's left to see them but the skulls.

Rain clouds threaten. Lightning blooms, and the battle-field goes monochrome. Thunder rolls. There will be rain tonight, to slick the glass that was the ground, if the planet lasts so long.

The letter's cinders die.

The shadow of a broken gunship twists. Empty, it fills.

A seeker emerges from that shadow, bearing other shadows with her.

Wordless, the seeker regards the aftermath. She does not weep, that anyone can see. She paces through the wrecks, over the bodies, professional: She works a winding spiral, ensuring with long-practiced arts that no one has followed her through the silent paths she walked to reach this place.

The ground shakes and shatters.

She reaches what was once a letter. Kneeling, she stirs the ashes. A spark flies up, and she catches it in her hand.

She removes a thin white slab from a pouch at her side and slips it under the ashes, spreads them thin against the white. Removes her glove, and slits her finger. Rainbow blood wells and falls and splatters into gray.

She works her blood into the ash to make a dough, kneads that dough, rolls it flat. All around, decay proceeds. The battleships become mounds of moss. Great guns break.

She applies jeweled lights and odd sounds. She wrinkles time.

The world cracks through the middle.

The ash becomes a piece of paper, with sapphire ink in a viny hand at the top.

This letter was meant to be read once, then destroyed.

In the moments before the world comes apart, she reads it again.

Look on my works, ye mighty, and despair!

A little joke. Trust that I have accounted for all variables of irony. Though I suppose if you're unfamiliar with overanthologized works of the early Strand 6 nineteenth century, the joke's on me.

I hoped you'd come.

You're wondering what this is—but not, I think, wondering who this is. You know—just as I've known, since our eyes met during that messy matter on Abrogast-882—that we have unfinished business.

I shall confess to you here that I'd been growing complacent. Bored, even, with the war; your Agency's flash and dash upthread and down, Garden's patient planting and pruning of strands, burrowing into time's braid. Your unstoppable force to our immovable object; less a game of Go than a game of tic-tac-toe, outcomes determined from the first move, endlessly iterated until the split where we fork off into unstable, chaotic possibility—the future we seek to secure at each other's expense.

But then you turned up.

My margins vanished. Every move I'd made by rote I had to bring myself to fully. You brought some depth to your side's speed, some staying power, and I found myself working at capacity again. You invigorated your Shift's war effort and, in so doing, invigorated me.

Please find my gratitude all around you.

I must tell you it gives me great pleasure to think of you reading these words in licks and whorls of flame, your eyes unable to work backwards, unable to keep the letters on a page; instead you must absorb them, admit them into your memory. In order to recall them you must seek my presence in your thoughts, tangled among them like sunlight in water. In order to report my words to your superiors you must admit yourself already infiltrated, another casualty of this most unfortunate day.

This is how we'll win.

It is not entirely my intent to brag. I wish you to know that I respected your tactics. The elegance of your work makes this war seem like less of a waste. Speaking of which, the hydraulics in your spherical flanking gambit were truly superb. I hope you'll take comfort from the knowledge that they'll be

thoroughly digested by our mulchers, such that our
next victory against your side will have a little piece
of you in it.

Better luck next time, then.

Fondly,

Blue

———————————————————————————

A glass jar of water boils in an MRI machine. In defiance of proverbs, Blue watches it.

When Blue wins—which is always—she moves on to the next thing. She savours her victories in retrospect, between missions, recalls them only while travelling (upthread into the stable past or downthread into the fraying future) as one recalls beloved lines of poetry. She combs or snarls the strands of time's braid with the finesse or brutality required of her, and leaves.

She is not in the habit of sticking around, because she is not in the habit of failing.

The MRI machine is in a twenty-first-century hospital, remarkably empty—evacuated, Blue observes—but never conspicuous to begin with, nestled in the green heart of a forest bisected by borders.

The hospital was meant to be full. Blue's job was a delicate matter of infection—one doctor in particular to intrigue with a new strain of bacteria, to lay the groundwork for twisting her world towards or away from biological warfare, depending on how the other side responded to Garden's move. But the opportunity's vanished, the loophole closed, and the only thing there for Blue to find is a jar labeled READ BY BUBBLING.

So she lingers by the MRI machine, musing as she does on the agonies of symmetry recording the water's randomness—the magnetic bones settled like reading glasses on the thermodynamic face of the universe, registering each bloom and burst of molecule before it transforms. Once it translates the last of the water's heat into numbers, she takes the printout in her right hand and fits the key of it into the lock of the letter-strewn sheet in her left.

She reads, and her eyes widen. She reads, and the data get harder to extract from the depth of her fist's clench. But she laughs, too, and the sound echoes down the hospital's empty halls. She is unaccustomed to being thwarted. Something about it tickles, even as she meditates on how to phase-shift failure into opportunity.

Blue shreds the data sheet and the cipher text, then picks up a crowbar.

In her wake, a seeker enters the hospital room's wreck, finds the MRI machine, breaks into it. The jar of water is cool. She tips its tepid liquid down her throat.

My most insidious Blue,

How does one begin this sort of thing? It's been so long since I last started a new conversation. We're not so isolated as you are, not so locked in our own heads. We think in public. Our notions inform one another, correct, expand, reform. Which is why we win.

Even in training, the other cadets and I knew one other as one knows a childhood dream. I'd greet comrades I thought I'd never met before, only to find we'd already crossed paths in some strange corner of the cloud before we knew who we were.

So: I am not skilled in taking up correspondence. But I have scanned enough books, and indexed enough examples, to essay the form.

Most letters begin with a direct address to the reader. I've done that already, so next comes shared business: I'm sorry you couldn't meet the good doctor. She's important. More to the point, her sister's children will be, if she visits them this afternoon and they discuss patterns in birdsong—which she will have done already by the time you decipher this note. My cunning methods for spiriting her from your clutches? Engine trouble, a good spring day, a suspiciously effective and cheap remote-access software suite her hospital purchased two years ago, which allows the good doctor to work from home. Thus we braid Strand 6 to Strand 9, and our glorious crystal future shines so bright I gotta wear shades, as the prophets say.

Remembering our last encounter, I thought it best to ensure you'd twist no other groundlings to your purpose, hence the bomb threat. Crude, but effective.

I appreciate your subtlety. Not every battle's grand, not every weapon fierce. Even we who fight wars through time forget the value of a word in the right moment, a rattle in the right car engine, a nail in the right horseshoe . . . It's so easy to crush a planet that you may overlook the value of a whisper to a snowbank.

Address the reader—done. Discuss shared business—done, almost.

I imagine you laughing at this letter, in disbelief. I have seen you laugh, I think—in the Ever Victorious Army's ranks, as your dupes burned the Summer Palace and I rescued what I could of the Emperor's marvelous clockwork devices. You marched scornful and fierce through the halls, hunting an agent you did not know was me.

So I imagine fire glinting off your teeth. You think you've wormed inside me—planted seeds or spores in my brain—whatever vegetal metaphor suits your fancy. But here I've repaid your letter with my own. Now we have a correspondence. Which, if your superiors discover it, will start a chain of questions I anticipate you'll find uncomfortable. Who's infecting whom? We know from our hoarse Trojans, in my time. Will you respond, establishing complicity, continuing our self-destructive paper trail, just to get in the last word? Will you cut off, leaving my note to spin its fractal math inside you?

I wonder which I'd rather.

Finally: conclude.

This was fun.

My regards to the vast and trunkless legs of stone,

Red

Red puzzles through a labyrinth of bones.

Other pilgrims wander here, in saffron robes or home-spun brown. Sandals shuffle over rocks, and high winds whistle around cave corners. Ask the pilgrims how the labyrinth came to be, and they offer answers varied as their sins. Giants made it, this one claims, before the gods slew the giants, then abandoned Earth to its fate at mortal hands. (Yes, this is Earth—long before the ice age and the mammoth, long before academics many centuries downthread will think it possible for the planet to have spawned pilgrims, or labyrinths. Earth.) The first snake built the labyrinth, says another, screwing down through rock to hide from the judgment of the sun. Erosion made it, says a third, and the grand dumb motion of tectonic plates, forces too big for we cockroaches to conceive, too slow for mayfly us to observe.

They pass among the dead, under chandeliers of shoulder

blades, rose windows outlined by rib cages. Metacarpals outline looping flowers.

Red asks the other pilgrims nothing. She has her mission. She takes care. She should meet no opposition as she makes a small twist this far upthread. At the labyrinth's heart there is a cavern, and soon into that cavern will come a gust of wind, and if that wind whistles over the right fluted bones, one pilgrim will hear the cry as an omen that will drive him to renounce all worldly goods and retreat to build a hermitage on a distant mountain slope, so that hermitage will exist in two hundred years to shelter a woman fleeing with child in a storm, and so it goes. Start a stone rolling, so in three centuries you'll have an avalanche. Little flash to such an assignment, less challenge, so long as she stays on script. Not even a taunt to disturb her path.

Did her adversary—did Blue—ever read her letter? Red liked writing it—winning tastes sweet, but sweeter still to triumph and tease. To dare reprisal. Every op since, she's watched her back, moved with double caution, waiting for payback, or for Commandant to find her small breach of discipline and bring the scourge. Red has her excuses ready: Since her disobedience she's been a better agent, more meticulous.

But no reply has come.

Perhaps she was wrong. Perhaps her enemy does not care, after all.

The pilgrims follow guides down the path of wisdom. Red departs and wanders narrow, twisting passages in the dark.

Darkness does not bother her. Her eyes do not work like normal eyes. She scents the air, and olfactory analytics flash into her brain, offering a trail. At a particular niche, she draws from her satchel a small tube that sheds red light on the skeletons arrayed within. The first time she does this, she finds nothing. The second, her light glints off a pulsing stripe on this femur, that jaw.

Satisfied, she adds femur and jaw to her bag, then banishes the light and wanders deeper down.

Imagine her in utter night, invisible. Imagine the footsteps, one by one, that never tire, never slip on cave dust or gravel. Imagine the precision with which her head swivels on her thick neck, swinging a measured arc from side to side. Hear (you can, just) gyroscopes whir in her gut, lenses click beneath the camouflage jelly of those pure black eyes.

She moves as fast as possible, within operating parameters.

More red lights. More bones join the others in the sack. She does not need to check her watch. A timer ticks down in the corner of her vision.

When she thinks she's found the bones she needs, she descends.

Far below the path of wisdom, the masters of this dark

place ran out of corpses. The niches remain, waiting—perhaps for Red.

Even the niches stop, eventually.

Soon after that, guards set upon her: eyeless giants grown by the sharp-toothed mistresses of this place. The giants' nails are yellow, thick, and cracked, and their breath smells better than one might expect.

Red breaks them quickly and quietly. She has no time for the less violent approach.

When she can no longer hear their moans, she reaches the cavern.

She knows by the changed echoes of her footsteps that she has found the place. When she kneels and stretches forth her hand, she feels ten centimeters of remaining ledge, then the abyss. Strong cold wind gusts past her: the Earth's own breath, or some great monster's far below. It howls. The noise clatters off the bone mobiles the nuns make down here, to remind themselves of the impermanence of flesh. The bones sing and turn, hanging from marrow twine in the darkness.

Red feels her way along the ledge until she finds one of the great anchored tree trunks from which the mobiles hang. She shimmies out upon the trunk until she reaches the bones of some ancient nun, hung by some other.

The countdown clock in her eye warns her how little time is left.

She cuts the old bones free with her diamond-sharp nails and takes her replacements from her pack. Strings them one by one with marrow twine, connecting skull and fibula, jaw and sternum, coccyx and xiphoid process.

The timer ticks down. Seven. Six.

She ties the knots rapidly, by touch. Her limbs inform her that they ache where they clutch this ancient trunk above an unfathomable drop.

Three. Two.

She lets the bones fall into the pit.

Zero.

A rush of wind splits the earth, a roar in darkness. Red clutches the petrified trunk closer than a lover. The wind peaks, screams, tosses bones about. A new note rises above the ossuary clatter, woken by the cavern's wind whistling over precise fluted pits in the bones Red has hung. The note grows, shifts, and swells into a voice.

Red listens, teeth bared in an expression that, if she saw it mirrored, she could not name. There's awe there, yes, and fury. What else?

She scans the lightless cavern. She detects no heat signature, no movement, no radar ping, no EM emissions or cloud trail—of course not. She feels gloriously exposed. Ready for the gunshot or the moment of truth.

Too soon, the wind dies, and the voice with it.

Red curses into the silence. Remembering the era, she invokes local fertility deities, frames inventive methods for their copulation. She exhausts her invective arsenal and growls, wordless, and spits into the abyss.

After all that, as prophesied, she laughs. Thwarted, bitter, but still, there's humor in it.

Before she leaves, Red saws free the bones she hung. The pilgrim Red meant to shape is gone, and the hermitage will be unbuilt. Now Red will have to fix the mess to the best of her ability.

The abandoned bones tumble and tumble and fall and fall.

But don't worry. The seeker catches them before they land.

Dear Red, in Tooth, in Claw,

You were right that I laughed. Your letter was very welcome. It told me a great deal. You imagined the fire glinting off my teeth; knowing your fine attention to detail, I thought I'd put a little devil in it.

Perhaps I ought to begin with an apology. This is not, I'm afraid, the omen you were anticipating; while you listen to my words, you might give a little thought to whose bones are cored and pocked with this letter. That poor pilgrim who might have been! Why leave a self-destructing paper trail when one can enjoy an asset-destroying scrimshaw session and let the wind take a turn tickling some ivory?

Don't worry—he lived a fine life first. Not the life you would have wanted for him, perhaps— unhappy but useful to posterity, harbouring the vulnerable, dimpling the future's punch cards one new life at a time. Instead of building a hermitage, he fell in love! Made glorious music with his fellow, travelled widely, drew tears from an emperor, melted her hard heart, bumped history out of one groove and into another. Strand 22 crosses Strand 56, if I'm not mistaken, and somewhere down-thread a bud's bloomed bright enough to taste.

It flatters me to find you so attentive. Be assured that I'll have looked long and hard at you while you assembled my little art project. Will you go still or turn sharply when you know that I'm watching you? Will you see me? Imagine me waving, in case you don't; I'll be too far off for you to see my mouth.

Just kidding. I'll be long gone by the time the wind turns right. Made you look, though, didn't I?

I imagine you laughing too.

I look forward to your reply,

Blue

———————————————————————

Blue approaches the temple in pilgrim's guise: hair shorn to show the shine of circuitry curling around ears and up to scalp, eyes goggled, mouth a smear of chrome sheen, eyelids chrome hooded. She wears antique typewriter keys on her fingertips in veneration of the great god Hack, and her arms are braceleted in whorls of gold, silver, palladium, glinting brighter than bright against her dark skin.

Seen from overhead she is one of thousands, indistinguishable from the slow press of bodies shuffling towards the temple: a borehole in the centre of a vast, sun-baked pavilion. No one enters it: Such worshipful heat would wither their god on its silicon vine.

But inside is where she needs to be.

Blue drums her key-clapped fingers against one another with a dancer's precision. *A*, *C*, *G*, *T*, backwards and forwards, bifurcated, reunited. Their percussive rhythm sequences an airborne strain of malware she's been breeding for genera-tions, an organism spreading invisible tendrils through this society's neural network, harmless until executed.

She snaps her fingers. A spark flares between them.

The pilgrims—all ten thousand of them, all at once—collapse, perfectly silent, into one vast ornamented heap.

She listens to the hiss and pop of overheated circuits misfiring in filigreed brains and walks peacefully through the incapacitated pilgrims, their twitching limbs like surf lapping softly at her ankles.

It amuses Blue to no end that, in disabling their temple, in mounting this attack, she has, herself, performed an act of devotion to their god.

She has ten minutes to navigate the temple labyrinth: down the service ladder hand over hand, then one palm against the dry, dark wall to follow its broken lines to a centre. It's cold underground, colder on her bare skin, colder still the deeper she goes, and she shivers but doesn't slow.

At the centre is a boxy screen. It lights up as Blue approaches.

"Hello, I'm Mackint—"

"Hush, Siri. I'm here for the riddles."

Eyes and a mouth—it can't quite be called a face—animate the screen, regard her evenly. "Very well. How do you calculate the hypotenuse of a right triangle?"

Blue tilts her head, stands very still, except for the flexing of her fingers at her side. She clears her throat.

"''Twas brillig, and the slithy toves / Did gyre and gimble in the wabe.' . . ."

Siri's screen blinks with static before it asks, "What is the value of pi to sixty-two decimals?"

"'The sedge is withered from the lake, / And no birds sing.'"

A fistful of snow skitters across Siri's face. "If train A leaves Toronto at six p.m. travelling east at one hundred kilometres per hour, and train B leaves Ottawa at seven p.m. travelling west at one hundred twenty kilometres per hour, when will they cross?"

"'Lo! the spell now works around thee, / And the clankless chain hath bound thee; / O'er thy heart and brain together / Hath the word been pass'd—now wither!'"

A flash of light: Siri powers down.

"Further," Blue adds, stepping lightly towards the box, making to lift it into the heavy bag next to it, "Ontario sucks. As the prophets say."

The screen flashes again; she steps back, startled. Words scroll across the screen, and as they do, her eyes widen, and the screen's blue-white light catches on the chrome paint of her mouth as it spreads, slowly, into a ferocious grin.

She clacks her keys one final time before shedding them from her fingers, the sheen from her mouth, the metal from her arms. As she steps sideways into the braid, the heap of ornament shrivels, rusts, flakes, indistinguishable from the fine grit of the cavern floor. The seeker, following after, distinguishes every grain.

Dearest Blue-da-ba-dee,

A daring intrusion! Mad props. I never would have believed your party would risk working Strand 8827 this far downthread until I recognized your distinctive signature. I shudder to imagine an equal and opposite incursion—may causality forbid Commandant ever dispatch me to one of your viny-hivey elfworlds, profusely floral, all arcing elder trees, neural pollen, bees gathering memories from eyes and tongue, honey libraries dripping knowledge from the comb. I harbor no illusions I'd succeed. You would find me in an instant, crush me faster—I'd walk a swath of rot through your verdancy, no matter how light I tried to step. I have a Cherenkov-green thumb.

(I know, I know: Cherenkov radiation's . . . well . . . blue. Never let facts break a good joke.)

But you're subtle. I barely heard the signs of your approach—I won't tell you what they were, for reasons you'll understand. Imagine me, if you want, crouched atop a stairwell, knees to chin, out of sight, counting the burglar's footfalls as she climbs. You're not half-bad at this. Did they grow you for this purpose? How does your side handle this sort of thing, anyway? Did they engender you knowing what you'd be; did they train you, run you through your paces at what I can only picture as some sort of horrific summer camp under the watchful eyes of concerned counselors who smile all the time?

Did your bosses send you here? Do you even have bosses? Or a queen? Might someone in your chain of command want to do you wrong?

I ask because we could have trapped you here. This strand's a prominent tributary; Commandant could field a swarm of agents without much causal risk. I imagine you reading this, thinking you would have escaped them all. Maybe.

But those agents are busy elsewhere, and it would be a waste of time (ha!) to recall them and dispatch again. Rather than bother Commandant with something I could handle on my own, I interceded directly. Easier for us both.

Of course, I couldn't let you steal these poor peoples' god. We don't need this place in specific, but we need something like it. I'm sure you can picture the work required to rebuild such a paradise from scratch (or even recover its gleam from the wreckage). Think, for a second—if you succeeded, if you stole the physical object on whose slow quantum decomposition this strand's random-number generators depend, if that triggered a cryptographic crisis, if that crisis led people to distrust their food printers, if hungry masses rioted, if riots fed this glitter to the fires of war, we'd have to start again—cannibalizing other strands, likely from your braid. And then we'd be at one another's throats even more.

Plus, this way I can repay you for that trick in the catacombs—with a note of my own! But I'm almost out of room. You like the Strand 6 nineteenth century. Well, *Mrs. Leavitt's Guide to Etiquette and Correspondence* (London, Gooseneck Press, Strand 61) suggests I should end by recapitulating my letter's main thrust, whatever that means, so, here goes: Ha-ha, Blueser. Your mission objective's in another castle.

Hugs and kisses,

Red

PS. The keyboard's coated with slow-acting contact poison. You'll be dead in an hour.

PPS. Just kidding! Or . . . am I?

PPPS. I'm just screwing with you. But postscripts sure are fun!

———————————————————————

Trees fall in the forest and make sounds.

The horde moves among them, judging, swinging axes, bowing bass notes from pine trunks with saws. Five years back, none of these warriors had seen such a forest. In their home stand sacred groves were called *zuun mod*, which means "one hundred trees," because one hundred were all the trees they thought might be gathered in one place.

Many more than a hundred trees stand here, a quantity so vast no one dares number it. Wet, cold wind spills down the mountains, and branches clatter like locust wings. Warriors creep beneath needled shadows and go about their work.

Icicles drip and snap as the great trees fall, and felled, the trees leave gaps in green that bare the cold white sky. Warriors like those flat clouds better than the forest's gloom, but not so much as they loved the blue of home. They loop the trunks with cord and drag them through trampled underbrush to the camp, where they will be peeled and planed to build the great Khan's war machines.

A strange transformation, some feel: When they were young, they won their first battles with bows, from horseback, ten men against twenty, two hundred against three. Then they learned to use rivers against their foes, to tear down their walls with grappling hooks. These days they roll from town to town collecting scholars, priests, and engineers, everyone who can read or write, who knows a trade, and set them tasks. You will have food, water, rest, all the luxury an army on hoof can offer. In exchange, solve the problems our enemies pose.

Once, horsemen broke on fortifications like waves against a cliff. (Most of these men have not seen waves, or cliffs, but travelers bear stories from distant lands.) Now the horsemen slaughter foes, drive them to their forts, demand surrender, and, should surrender not ensue, they raise up their engines to undo the knot of the city.

But those engines need lumber, so off the warriors are sent, to steal from ghosts.

Red, hard-ridden for days, dismounts within the wood. She wears a thick gray del belted with silk around her waist, and a fur hat covers her hair, preserving her scalp from the chill. She walks heavily. She broadens her shoulders. She has played this role for at least a decade. Women ride with the horde—but she is a man now, so far as those who give her orders, and follow hers in turn, are concerned.

She commits the enterprise to memory for her report. Her breath smokes, glitters as ice crystals freeze. Does she miss steam heat? Does she miss walls and a roof? Does she miss the dormant implants sewn through her limbs and tangled in her chest that could shore her against this cold, stop her feeling, seal a force field around her skin to guard her from this time to which she's been sent?

Not really.

She notes the deep green of the trees. She measures the timing of their fall. She records the white of the sky, the bite of the wind. She remembers the names of the men she passes. (Most of them are men.) Ten years into deep cover, having joined the horde, proven her worth, and achieved the place for which she strove, she feels suited to this war.

She has suited herself to it.

Others draw back from her in respect and fear as she scans the piled logs for signs of rot. Her roan snorts, stamps the earth. Red ungloves and traces the lumber with her fingertips, log by log, ring by ring, feeling each one's age.

She stops when she finds the letter.

Kneels.

The others gather round: What has disturbed her so? An omen? A curse? Some flaw in their lumberjackery?

The letter begins in the tree's heart. Rings, thicker here

and thinner there, form symbols in an alphabet no one present knows but Red. The words are small, sometimes smudged, but still: ten years per line of text, and many lines. Mapping roots, depositing or draining nutrients year by year, the message must have taken a century to craft. Perhaps local legends tell of some fairy or frozen goddess in these woods, seen for an instant, then gone. Red wonders what expression she wore as she placed the needle.

She memorizes the message. She feels it ridge by ridge, line by line, and performs a slow arithmetic of years.

Her eyes change. The men nearby have known her for a decade but have never seen her look like this.

One asks, "Should we throw it away?"

She shakes her head. It must be used. She does not say, Or else another might find it and read what I have read.

They drag the logs to camp. They split them, trim them, plane them, frame them into engines of war. Two weeks later, the planks lie shattered around the fallen walls of a city still burning, still weeping. Progress gallops on, and blood remains behind.

Vultures circle, but they've feasted here already.

The seeker crosses the barren land, the broken city. She gathers splinters from the engines' wrecks, and as the sun sets, she slides those splinters one by one into her fingers.

Her mouth opens, but she makes no sound.

My perfect Red,

How many boards would the Mongols hoard if the Mongol horde got bored? Perhaps you'll tell me once you're finished with this strand.

The thought that you could have trapped me (stranded me, perhaps? Oh dear, sorry-not-sorry) is so delicious that I confess myself quite over-come. Do you always play things safe, then? Run the numbers so precisely that you can reject out of hand any scenario that has a projected success rate of less than 80 percent? It grieves me to think you'd make a boring poker player.

But then I imagine you'd cheat, and that's a comfort.

(I'd never want you to let me win. The very idea!)

I wore goggles, but imagine, please, the widen-ing of my eyes at your sweet interrogation in Strand 8827. Did my bosses send me there! Do I have bosses! A suggestion of corruption in my command chain! A charming concern for my well-being! Are you trying to recruit me, dear Cochineal?

"And then we'd be at each other's throats even more." Oh, petal. You say that like it's a bad thing.

It occurs to me to dwell on what a microcosm we are of the war as a whole, you and I. The physics of us. An action and an equal and opposite reaction. My viny-hivey elfworld, as you say, versus your techy-mechy dystopia. We both know it's nothing so simple, any more than a letter's reply is its opposite. But which egg preceded what platypus? The ends don't always resemble our means.

But enough philosophy. Let me tell you what you have told me, speaking plain: You could have killed me, but didn't. You have acted without the knowledge or sanction of your Agency. Your vision of life in Garden is sufficiently full of silly stereotypes to read as a calculated attempt at provoking a stinging, unguarded response (hilarious, given how long it took me to grow these words), but spoken with such keen beauty as to suggest a confession of real, curious ignorance.

(We do have superb honey: best eaten in a thickness of comb, spread on warm bread with soft cheese, in a cool part of the day. Do your kind eat anymore? Is it all tubes and intravenous nutrition, metabolisms optimised for far-strand food? Do you sleep, Red, or dream?)

Let me also speak plain, before this tree runs out of years, before the fine fellows under your command make siege weapons of my words: What do you want from this, Red? What are you doing here?

Tell me something true, or tell me nothing at all.

Best,

Blue

PS. I'm touched by the research effort expended on my behalf. *Mrs. Leavitt's Guide* is a good one. Now that you've discovered postscripts, I look forward to what you could do with scented inks and seals!

PPS. There's no trick here, no thwart. Give my best to this strand's Genghis. We lay on our backs and watched clouds together when we were young.

Blue sees her chosen name reflected everywhere around her: moon-slicked floes, ocean thick with drift ice, liquid churned to glass. She munches a piece of dry biscuit on deck while the ship's hands sleep, dusts the crumbs off her mitts, and watches them fall into the white-flecked pitch of the waters.

The schooner's name is *The Queen of Ferryland*, carrying a full complement of hunters eager to stack scalps in the hold, hungry for what fur and flesh and fat will buy them in the off-season. Blue's interest is partly in oil, but chiefly in the deployment of new steam technologies: There is a staggering of outcomes to achieve, a point off which to tip the industry, a rudder with which to steer these ships between the Scylla of one doom and the Charybdis of another, onto a course that leads to Garden.

Seven strands tangle on the collapse or survival of this

fishery—insignificant to some eyes, everything to others. Some days Blue wonders why anyone ever bothered making numbers so small; other days she supposes even infinity needs to start somewhere.

Those days rarely happen while on a mission.

Who can speak of what Blue thinks on a mission, when missions are often whole lives, when the story spun for her to wield a hunter's hook is years in the making? So many roles, dresses, parties, trousers, intimacies rolled into grasping a berth and bundling into shapeless clothes to keep Newfoundland's winter at bay.

The horizon blinks, and morning yawns above it. Hunters spill over the schooner's side, Blue among them: They sweep across the ice, tools in hand, laughing, singing, striking skulls and splitting skins.

Blue has hauled three skins on board when a big, brash beater catches her eye: It raises its head in threat for all of half a second before bolting for the water. Blue is faster. The beater's skull breaks like an egg beneath her club. She drops into a crouch beside it to inspect the pelt.

The sight hits her like a hakapik. There, in the ice-rimed fur, mottled and marked as hand-pulped paper, spots and speckles resolve into a word she can read: "Blue."

Her hand does not shake as she slices into the skin. Her breath comes even. She's kept her gloves clean, for the most part, but now she stains them red as a name.

Buried in the depths of glistening viscera is a dry piece of cod, undigested, scratched and grooved with language. She hardly realises that she's settled her body onto the ice, cross-legged, comfortable, as if tea, not seal guts, steamed dark and fragrant beside her.

She'll keep the pelt. The cod she'll crush to powder, sprinkle over rancidly buttered biscuit and eat for dinner; the body she'll dispose of in the usual way.

When the seeker comes hard and fast on her trail, all that's left is a smear of dark red on blue snow. On hands and knees, she licks and sucks and chews until all the colour's gone.

My Dear Mood Indigo,

I apologize for, well, everything. It's been a long time from my perspective, and, I'm afraid, yours, since your letter—I had another decade or so with Genghis (who says hi, by the way—he told me the most interesting stories about you, or, I assume it was you), after-action reports following, and after those I had the usual sort of routine rebraiding dance. An assessment wrapped the whole thing up. I passed—as ever. The usual nonsense. I imagine you have something of the same: The Agency squats far downthread, issues agents up; then Commandant doubts the agents who return. Yes, we diverge in our travels; yes, we acquire shades; we round; we behave asocially. Adaption is the price of victory. You might think they would realize that.

I spent the better part of a year recovering from your so-called sense of humor. Hordes and boards!

I consulted the literature on scents and wax seals, as you suggested. It's all a bit counterintuitive, this business of communication through base matter. Closing a letter—a physical object without even a ghost in the cloud, all that data on one frail piece of paper—with an even more malleable substance, bearing, of all things, an ideographic signature! Informing any handler of the message's sender, her role, perhaps even her purpose! Madness—from an operational-security perspective. But, as the prophets say, there ain't no mountain high enough—so I've essayed the work here. I hope you enjoy your whacked seal. I didn't supply any extra scent, but the medium has a savor all its own.

There's a kind of time travel in letters, isn't there? I imagine you laughing at my small joke; I imagine you groaning; I imagine you throwing my words away. Do I have you still? Do I address empty air and the flies that will eat this carcass? You could leave me for five years, you could return never—and I have to write the rest of this not knowing.

I prefer read-receipts, all things considered—the instant handshake of slow telepathy through our wires. But this is a fascinating technology, in its limits.

You ask if we eat.

It's a hard question to answer. There is no

mono-we; there are many usses. The usses change and interleave. Have you ever stared into the workings of a watch? I'm talking about a really, really good watch—if you want to see what I mean, climb downthread to thirty-third-century-CE Ghana. Limited Unlimited in Accra does wonderful pieces with translucent nanoscale gears, no larger than grains of sand, teeth invisibly small, actions and counteractions and complications: They break light like a kaleidoscope. And they keep good time. There's one of you, but so many of us—pieces layered atop pieces, each with its own traits, desires, purposes. One person may wear different faces in different rooms. Minds swap bodies for sport. Everyone is anything they want. The Agency imposes a modicum of order. So, do we eat?

I do.

I don't need to. We grow in pods, our basic knowledge flashed in cohort by cohort, nutrient balance maintained by the gel bath, and there most of us stay, our minds flitting disembodied through the void from star to star. We live through remotes, explore through drones—the physical world but one of many, and uninteresting by comparison to most. Some do decant and wander, but they can sustain themselves for months on a charge, and there's always a pod to go back to when you want it.

All of this refers mostly to civilians, of course. Agents need more independent modes of operation. We are separate from the mass, and we move in our own bodies. It's easier that way.

Eating's gross, isn't it? In the abstract, I mean. When you're used to hyperspace recharging stations, to sunlight and cosmic rays, when most of the beauty you've known lies in a great machine's heart, it's hard to see the appeal of using bones that poke from spit-coated gums to mash things that grew in dirt into a paste that will fit down the wet tube connecting your mouth to the sack of acid under your heart. Takes the new recruits a long time to get used to, once they're decanted.

But I enjoy eating these days. More of us do than care to admit it publicly. I revel in it, as one only revels in pursuits one does not need. The runner enjoys running when she need not flee a lion. Sex improves when decoupled—sorry—from animalist procreative desperation (or even from the desperation of not having had sex in a while, as I've had cause to note after my recent two decades' sojourn and attendant dry spell).

I bite blueberry pancakes drizzled with maple syrup, extra butter—that expanding fluff, the berry's pop against my teeth, butter's bloom in my mouth. I explore sweetnesses and textures. I'm never hungry, so I don't race to the next bite. I eat glass, and as it cuts my gums, I savor minerals, metals, impurities; I see the beach from which some poor bastard skimmed the sand. Small rocks taste of the river, of rubbed fish scale, of glaciers long gone. They crunch, crisp, celery-like. I share the sensation with fellow aficionados; they share theirs with me, though there's lag, and sensor granularity remains an issue,

So, a roundabout way of saying: I love to eat.

Probably too much. I seldom can in public, back at the Agency. Commandant starts asking questions if you do. Jaunts upthread, to places where they eat *all the time*, feel decadent.

How about you? I don't mean, necessarily, how do you eat, though if you want to fill me in, be my guest. (Your descriptions of honey and bread—thank you for that.) I've described, a bit, our overlapping models—communities public and private, shared interests, shared senses. What's it like to be a part of yours? Do you have friends, Blue? And how?

You asked me to tell truths. I have. What do I want? Understanding. Exchange. Victory. A game— hiding and discovery. You're a swift opponent, Blue. You play long odds. You run the table. If we're to be at war, we might as well entertain one another. Why else did you taunt me at the start?

Yours,

Red

PS. Cochineal! I get it now.

Atlantis sinks.

Serves it right. Red hates the place. For one thing, there are so many Atlantises, always sinking, in so many strands: an island off Greece, a mid-Atlantic continent, an advanced pre-Minoan civilization on Crete, a spaceship floating north of Egypt, on and on. Most strands lack Atlantis altogether, know the place only through dreams and mad poets' madder whispers.

Because there are so many, Red cannot fix just one, or fail to. Sometimes it seems strands bud Atlantises to thwart her. They conspire. History makes common cause with the enemy. Thirty, forty times throughout her career she has walked away from some sinking, burning island, thinking, at least that's over. Thirty, forty times, the call has come: Go back.

At the foot of the volcano, the dark-skinned Atlanteans seek their ships. A mother carries her screaming son in one arm, clutches her daughter by the hand. Father follows. He bears their household gods. Tears streak the soot on his face. A priestess and a priest remain with their temple. They will be burned. They have lived their lives as sacrifices to—who again? Red has lost track. She feels bad about that.

They lived their lives as sacrifices.

Gods and children first, they fill the boats. As the earth shakes and the sky burns, even the bravest and most single-minded leave their work. Notes and sums and new engines remain behind. They take people and art. The math will burn, the engines melt, the arches fall to dust.

This is not even one of the weirder Atlantises. No crystals here, no flying cars, no perfect governments, no psychic powers. (Those last two things don't exist, anyway.) And yet: That man built a steam-and-pinwheel engine six centuries earlier than the mean. This woman, through reason and ecstatic meditation, discerned the usefulness of zero to her mathematics. This shepherd built freestanding arches into the walls of his house. Small touches, ideas so fundamental they seem useless. Nobody here knows their worth, yet. But if they do not perish on this island, someone might realize their use a few centuries earlier and change everything.

So Red tries to give them time.

Her implants glow bright crimson to vent heat. They sear her flesh. She sweats buckets. Growls. Glowers. She pushes herself, here. Island saving's not a one-woman job, so she works harder than one woman can.

She rolls enormous boulders to break the coming lava flows. She plows new fake riverbeds with her hands. With the tools at her disposal she breaks rocks and forms their pieces into other rocks elsewhere. The volcano quakes and splits, vomits rock into the air. A stone pine of soot sprouts from its peak. She sprints uphill, a streak of skin and light.

The lava shimmers, bubbles, spits. Some lands near her. She steps aside.

The ash-green sea reflects the roil-black sky. The last cormorants flee, darkness against dark. Red searches for a sign. She is missing something. She does not know what. She ponders skies and oceans for a while, wonders.

While Red looks away, a gob of lava splashes toward her face. She catches it in her palm without looking. Her skin, if it were the sort of skin the panicked villagers below wear around their meat, should char. It is not, does not.

Too long watching. She turns back to the caldera, to the welling lava.

She stops.

Black and gold vein the rising red. Some suns' surfaces look like this, when she visits them on shore leave. That's not what arrests her.

The shifting colors form words that last mere moments, in

handwriting now familiar. As the lava flows, those words change.

She reads. Her lips frame syllables one by one. She commits the words the fire frames to the old kind of memory. There are cameras in her eyes, which she does not use for this. A recording mechanism clamps around the strand of fiber in her skull which might be mistaken for an optic nerve; she turns it off, which the Agency does not think she can do. The lava overflows its lip. She had meant to break this high promontory on which she stands, to make a sort of spout, spilling molten rock down her predetermined channel. Rather, she stands and watches.

Below, the village burns. Without her capstone effort at the peak, her dikes and redoubts work less well, but the mathematician still has time to grab her wax tablets at least. The boats leave. They get far enough away to survive the earthquake wave as their homes tumble into the sea.

Red has not quite failed. She shakes her head and walks away, hoping this is the last Atlantis they will send her back to save. She remembers.

The volcano stills. Winds part the clouds, in time, and leave the sky blue.

The seeker scrambles up the slick and barren hill. Strands of thin, glistening volcanic glass cluster near the cooling lava. In another time and place they will be called Pele's Hair. The seeker gathers them by hand, like flowers, humming.

My careful Cardinal—

Let me tell you a secret: I loathe Atlantis. Every last single Atlantis across all strands. It's a putrid thread. Everything you've likely been taught about Garden and my Shift should lead you to believe we treasure it as a bastion of good works, the original Platonic ideal for how a civilisation ought to be: How many bright-eyed adolescents have poured the fervour of their souls into lives imagined there? Magic! Infinite wisdom! Unicorns! The gods themselves made flesh! The work we do to maintain these notions is more subtle than you might think, given the publishing peccadilloes of a dozen twentieth centuries. What a robust priesthood Atlantis must have had to support so many earnest young things pitching their past lives in its temples!

But what a dreary place. Stagnant, sick as a sucking wound. A successful experiment with disgusting results. The volcano was the best thing to ever happen to it: Now it's legend, possibility, mystery, a far more generative engine than anything it developed over a few thousand years.

That's what we treasure. That's us, always: the volcano and the wave.

Thank you for your words on eating. After weeks of ship's biscuit they were especially welcome. I should tell you, as Mrs. Leavitt would, that it's customary to send letters that can be opened without ruining the seal, but I appreciate your innovation more than I can say.

What I can say: It was very cold out on the ice. Your letter warmed me.

Your talk of ideographic signatures and operational security brought to mind some grooming work I did among a few strands' worth of Bess of Hardwick's botanists. While there it was my pleasure to observe correspondence between them and their Lady; just how layered and complex plain speech could be, how many secrets wrapped in the banner of Sincerity (a word commonly invented in sixteenth centuries). Even that ideographic signature could easily be a lie, of course: counterfeit stamps, sealed letters hidden under separate cover, the wrong colour of wax or silk flossing. How much glorious double-talk took place while Mary, Queen of Scots, was under her roof! I assure you that cryptography pales in comparison; imagine a cipher made up of interlocking moods shifting in response to environmental stimuli.

Also, standardized spelling wasn't yet a feature of English. Forging someone's handwriting was wasted effort if you didn't also learn their idiosyncratic orthography. Funnily enough, that would prove to be the undoing of latter-century forgers. Chatterton, that Marvellous Boy, et cetera.

We make so much of lettercraft literal, don't we? Whacked seals aside. Letters as time travel, time-travelling letters. Hidden meanings.

I wonder what you see me saying here.

Absent from your mention of food—so sweet, so savoury—was any mention of hunger. You spoke of the lack of need, yes—no lion in pursuit, no "animalist procreative desperation," and these lead to enjoyment, certainly. But hunger is a many-splendoured thing; it needn't be conceived only in limbic terms, in biology. Hunger, Red—to sate a hunger or to stoke it, to feel hunger as a furnace, to trace its edges like teeth—is this a thing you, singly, know? Have you ever had a hunger that whetted itself on what you fed it, sharpened so keen and bright that it might split you open, break a new thing out?

Sometimes I think that's what I have instead of friends.

I hope it isn't too hard to read this. Best I could do on short notice—hope it reaches you before the island breaks around you.

Write to me in London next.

Blue

———————————————————

London Next—the same day, month, year, but one strand over—is the kind of London other Londons dream: sepia tinted, skies strung with dirigibles, the viciousness of empire acknowledged only as a rosy backdrop glow redolent of spice and petalled sugar. Mannered as a novel, filthy only where story requires it, all meat pies and monarchy—this is a place Blue loves, and hates herself for loving.

She sits in a Mayfair teahouse, in a corner, back to the wall with one eye on the door—some spycraft rules transcend both time and space—and the other on a stylised map of the New World. She finds it slightly incongruous—the teahouse favours a decidedly Orientalist aesthetic—but eclecticism is one of the many things Blue cherishes about the fibres of this particular strand.

Her hair now is black and thick and long, deftly styled into a high chignon girdled in braids, carefully twisted curls clustering at her nape, drawing attention to the length and slope of her neck. Her dress is modest and neat, not quite at the cutting edge of fashion; it's been a couple of years since the Princess line was new, but she suits it in charcoal grey. She is not here to play a role; she is here to be invisible.

She has observed, with pleasure, the very fine china of which the establishment boasts: Meissen's Ming Dragon, sinuous as arteries, persimmon bright against gilt-edged bone white. She looks forward to her own pot, anticipates the dark, smoky, malty path her chosen tea will pick between the notes of candied rose, delicate bergamot, champagne and muscat and violet.

Her server arrives, quietly, unobtrusively laying out the Meissen tiered cake tray, teapot, sugar bowl. As she settles the teacup on its saucer, however, Blue's hand snaps out to circle her retreating wrist. The server looks terrified.

"This set," says Blue, adjusting, softening her eyes into kindness, her grip into a caress, "is mismatched."

"I'm so sorry, miss," says the server, biting her lip. "I'd already made the pot, but the cup was cracked, and I thought you'd not want to wait longer for your tea, and all the other sets were spoken for on account of it's a busy time of day, but if you're happy to wait I could—"

"No," she says, and her smile is like clouds parting; the withdrawal of her hand into her lap is an erasure, a thing the server imagined, surely, this woman is a perfect picture of a lady, "it's very beautiful. Thank you."

The server ducks her head and retreats back into the kitchen. Blue stares intently at the teacup, its saucer and spoon: Blue Italian, classical figures harvesting grain, carrying water forever beneath the rim.

She pours her tea, delicately, without straining the leaves. She lifts her teaspoon to the light—can see that it's coated with a downthread substance she thinks she recognises but sniffs to be sure. She wills herself not to look around, commands every atom of her body into stillness, forbids the need to leap into the kitchen and pursue and hunt and catch—

Instead, she stirs the spoon, empty, into the tea, and watches as the leaves unclump, swirl, spindle into letters. Each rotation is slow, and she marks paragraph breaks with small sips; every sip undoes the letters until she swirls them into meaning again.

Briefly she wonders if the hardness in her throat is poison, her inability to swallow around it anaphylactic. This does not frighten her.

She closes her eyes against the alternative, which does.

When the tea and letter are finished, clumps remain; she reads the dregs as a postscript. Easy enough to do when the New World map matches it so precisely; easy to read the discrepancy as direction.

She dabs at her mouth, lifts the teacup, places it upside down beneath the boot of her heel, and grinds it so hard and swift that its destruction makes no sound.

After she's gone, the seeker, dressed as help, armed with dustpan and brush, collects the remnants, gathers them like rosebuds. When she is out of sight, she cuts the mix of clay and bone and leaf into three tidy lines, tightly rolls up a bank note, and inhales sharply enough to feel smoke behind her eyes.

Dearest 0000FF,

Common cause on Atlantis—who would have thought? I suppose no thread's one thing; they train us full confident in that knowledge. Each has facets, hooks, barbs, useful in different ways, depending on articulation. The novice believes a single change will make a thread thus, or thus. An event—an invasion or a spasm or a sigh—is like a hammer: one side blunt and perfect for driving nails, the other clawed to pry them free. And, like hammers, you store Atlantises out of sight when not in use: stick 'em in a drawer somewhere safe till the next need comes around.

I wonder, in that light, how much of your work has helped me, and the other way round—a question beyond my calculative capacity. I'd ask the Chaos Oracle, but I have enough trouble with the higher-ups at present. I had to step fast after your last letter caught me napping. Commandant wanted explanations, as Commandant tends to, after the sinking island took so many treasures with it. A brief lapse in efficiency, according to the Agency's models, but well within tolerance considering my track record. But added to the inroads your side's made against our more exposed deep-cover teams—well, I shouldn't talk shop. What a bore, your tea salon pals would say.

I summarize: It's been too long since my last letter.

Strand 233's Atlantis was not the most offensive of the brood, and I spent little enough time there. Joke as I might, I see the value. Humans need marks to strive for—but imperfect systems decay. So we build them ideals. Change agents climb upthread, find helpful strands, preserve what matters, and let what doesn't fall to dust: mulch for the more perfect future's seed.

Mrs. Leavitt suggests relying on metaphors one's correspondent—that's you, I think?—will find meaningful. I confess I don't entirely know what's meaningful to you. I fall back on assumptions: seeds and grass, growing things. It verges on stereotype. And when you write me, you write in furnace and in flame.

You ask about hunger.

You ask, in particular, about *my* hunger.

The short answer: no.

The longer answer: I don't think so?

We sate needs before they strike. In this body, an organ (a designed, implanted, rigorously tested organ) seated somewhere above my stomach registers the moment my metabolism requires fuel and stops the lizard-brained old subsystems that would make me keen and irritable and blunt my thoughts—all those tricks Dame Evolution plays to make us hunters, killers, seekers and finders and gorgers. I can disable the organ when I must, but it's so much more stable to receive a status report than to feel weak.

But the hunger you describe—that blade jutting from the skin, the weathering as of a hillside often struck by storm, the hollowness—it sounds beautiful and familiar.

When I was a girl, I loved reading. An archaic pastime, I know; the index and download are faster, more efficient, offering superior retention and acquisition of knowledge. But I read, antique volumes handed down and fresh-replicated books: How strange to uncover things in sequence! And so I read a comic book once, about Socrates. In the comic book, he was a soldier—he was, that part's true, I asked him—and one night, as his fellows lay down to sleep, he started thinking. He stood, immobile, lost in thought, until the dawn—at which instant he found the answer to his question.

It all seemed very romantic to me at the time. So I left my pod and wandered upthread and far away, far from the chatter and the mutual observation. I found a hilltop on a small world, breathable but barren, and I stood there like Socrates in the comic book, lost in thought, weight on one foot, and I did not move.

The sun set. The stars rose. (They are a rose, right? Or something? Dante said that.) I realized that as my ears grew used to the silence, I could still hear the others: Our chatter swarmed the heavens; our voices echoed from the stars. This was not how Socrates stood, or Li Bai or Qu Yuan either. My isolation, my experiment, had caused a small sensation among those who cared for me, and for whom I cared, and that sensation spread. Lenses and eyes turned upon me.

I was, I think, thirteen.

I received suggestions: philosophy textbooks, meditation guides, offers of practice and alliance. They crowded round. Whispers in my ears: *Are you okay? Do you need help? You can talk to us. You always can.*

There were tears. Other organs bind that process too, weeping—they keep our eyes clear and minds sharp, but chemistry is chemistry; cortisol, cortisol.

It feels harder to write than it should. It feels easier to write than it should, as well. I'm contradicting myself. The geometers would be ashamed.

I sent them away.

Each being's entitled to her privacy, so I refused to let them see me. I was the only person on that tiny rock, and I made the world go dark.

Wind blows. High places grow cold at night. Sharp rocks hurt my feet. For the first time in thirteen years I was alone. I, whatever I was, whatever I am, tumbled first up, into the stars, then down to the broken land. I dug into the soil. Night birds called; something like a wolf, but solitary and larger, with six legs and double-banked eyes, padded past.

The tears dried.

And I felt lonely. I missed those voices. I missed the minds behind them. I wanted to be seen. That need dug into the heart of me. It felt good. I'm not certain how to compare this to something you would know, but, imagine a person melded to a Thing, an artificial god the size of mountains, built for making war in the far corners of the cosmos. Imagine that great weight of metal all around her, pressing her down, giving her strength, its hoses melding with her flesh. Imagine she shears the hoses off, steps out: frail, sapped, weak, free.

I was light, hollowed, hungry. The sun rose. I found no revelation. I'm not Socrates. (I know Socrates, I served with Socrates, and you, senator . . . But I digress.) But I walked on, from that place to another, and from that to another in turn, until, years later, I came home.

And when Commandant found me, slid inside me, said, there's work for those like you, I wondered if all Agents were like me. They weren't—I found that later. But we're all deviant in our different ways.

Is that hunger? I don't know.

No friends, though? Blue! That's not at all what I would have thought. I don't know—I suppose we see you all curling around campfires singing old struggle songs.

Have you been lonely?

I hope the tea's well. Good? Well. I'll look for you next in a more public forum.

Yours,

Red

PS. I hesitate to write this, but—I've noticed my letters run long. If you'd rather I grow more concise, I can. I don't want to presume.

PPS. Apologies for the imprecision of my salutation—I think salutation's what Mrs. Leavitt calls that? I forgot what name the Strand 8 C19 Londoners gave that shade of blue on imported porcelain. Would have used it if I remembered.

PPPS. We're still going to win.

As the prophet says: Everybody's building them big ships and boats.

The emperor reigns uphill, flanked by his mummified co-rulers' temples, each served by their own high priest. Stone steps and highways link peak to peak along the ridge. Great cities grow and glow. Downslope spread the farms, and beneath those, against the shoreline, unprecedented as pomegranates in local logic, a seaport.

Coastline trade occurs, of course, and reed boats ply the highland lakes. Quechua sailors and fisherman know the shapes of the wind, can sail through any storm, rate themselves equal to any wave. The western ocean's horizon has always seemed a wall to them: Beyond this rests the world's end. But a genius who has spent his life counting the paths of stars and collecting bits of storm-cast wood and weed upon the beach has a theory that another land waits across the water. Another genius, a decade older than the first, has discovered a method for knotting reeds far stronger and more durable than any her mothers made; with it, a team under her direction could build a boat large enough to carry a village.

What good is a land across the water, young men asked the first genius, when we have no way to get there? As soon grasp for the moon.

What good for coastal fishing, young men asked the second, is a boat that can carry a village?

Fortunately, geniuses understand that young men are often fools.

So they sought the wisest being they knew: Each, separately, climbed the many thousand steps to the mountain peak, and on audience day they knelt before the current emperor's great-grandfather, mummified upon his throne, gold- and jewel-bedecked, radiant with age and command, and offered their gifts to him. And the secret priests who wait behind the emperor's thrones are not young, nor are they all men, and they can frame two points into a line.

So the great-grand-emperor's word goes out, and so a port is built, and sailors flock, beckoned by adventure. (Adventure works in any strand—it calls to those who care more for living than for their lives.) They will sail together, to a new world. They will sail, together, to a land of monsters and miracles. Currents will bear their massive fish-tailed ships across, freighted with silver and tapestries, with knot work and destiny.

Red knots reeds with fingers callused as wood. She was one of the second genius's earliest students, she nudged her to seek the great-grand-emperor's aid and held her elbow as they climbed. She is no warrior here, no general; she is a woman taller than usual, who emerged from the woods one day naked and alone and was sheltered. She knots and weaves well, because she has learned. When she has finished this ship, the production model, large enough to hold two villages at least—then it will sail, and she will sail with it, because someone needs to tend the knots if they break.

She plays a tenuous game, this strand. As she knots and thinks to herself, she decides she would describe it using terms from Go: You place each stone expecting it may do many things. A strike is also a block is also a different strike. A confession is also a dare is also a compulsion.

Will the people of Tawantinsuyu brave the ocean their murderers will one day call the Pacific, and, finding the swift currents, travel to the Philippines, or even farther, as others have traveled before? Will they, crossing waters so unfished that all a woman need do to eat is dart her hand beneath the waves and pull the fish up wriggling and silver, find new civilizations and make conquest, or common cause? Will this alliance and trade, stretched across the Pacific, save

Tawantinsuyu when Pizarro's grotesque sails belly up from the south? Will, at the least, early contact with Eurasian plagues strengthen these people against them?

Or: Will the tradesmen make it so far as a China ruled by the Ming, soon to reel from an enormous currency crisis that will bring the empire to its knees—a currency crisis brought on by the shifting exchange rate between copper cash and silver, of which the people of Tawantinsuyu sport an ample supply? Stabilized, will the Ming duck the four-century cycle of empires' rise and fall, and endure, growing, transforming, expanding to keep pace with the West's slow Enlightenment and its overweening Industrial Revolution?

Perhaps. Small likelihood—but we must seize each chance. The Agency is not happy. Other agents have been caught or killed, cleansed from the weave or marooned in strands of which it's better not to think. Not Red. Not yet. But she must work faster.

Red's hands slip on the knot. She is not thinking to herself. She is explaining. And to whom is she explaining? Well.

She looks out to the meeting of sky and sea.

Stands up.

Walks away.

She feels observed. Might Commandant be watching her? And if so, for what? She has been so careful. She does not even think the sky's name, often.

An old man catches her pacing on the beach and offers cloth for the sails: sample after sample. She flips through them: too weak, too weak, too weak, too rough, and this one—what even is it? Bunched and uneven, more crochet than weaving.

"This one," she says.

As the sun falls west, she perches on a rock and rolls the language of the knots between her oak-hard fingers. She feels each letter and word and wonders how long the sky and sea spent winding this cord, and who taught her the knot code in the first place, whether the iris bit her lip in frustration as she worked through a difficult passage.

When the sun's set, she takes the unraveled thread, snips it into lengths, and throws each length into the receding tide.

Stars shine, and the moon. A dark shape slips along bright waves and dives. One by one, the seeker gathers the strands and ties them about her wrist so tight her fingers pale and stiffen. She makes a fist, tenses. Her skin splits beneath the cord and closes over it again.

Red, who's waited motionless on the shore since sundown, sees something like a seal against the waves of light, and wonders.

Dear Red Sky at Morning,

Don't shorten your letters.

You ask if I've been lonely. I hardly know how to answer. I have observed friendship as one observes high holy days: breathtakingly short, whirlwinds of intimate endeavour, frenzied carousing, the sharing of food, of wine, of honey. Compressed, always, and gone as soon as they come. It is often my duty to fall in love convincingly, and certainly I've received no complaints. But that is work, and there are better things of which to write.

You say you were thirteen. You do not— You seem so young to me, still, however long ago that may seem like it was to you.

My own folk are great gardeners. Our games are long and slow, and our maturation also. Garden seeds the past with us—your Commandant knows this already, whether or not it's considered need-to-know for you—and we learn from and grow into its threads. We treat the past as trellis, coax our vineyard through and around, and harvest is not a word for swiftness; the future harvests us, stomps us into wine, pours us back into the root system in loving libation, and we grow stronger and more potent together.

I have been birds and branches. I have been bees and wolves. I have been ether flooding the void between stars, tangling their breath into networks of song. I have been fish and plankton and humus, and all these have been me.

But while I've been enmeshed in this wholeness—they are not the whole of me.

The thought of your disembodied network repulses me, but I look at you, Red, and see much of myself: a desire to be apart, sometimes, to understand who I am without the rest. And what I return to, the me-ness that I know as pure, inescapable self . . . is hunger. Desire. Longing, this longing to possess, to become, to break like a wave on a rock and reform, and break again, and wash away. This is a necessary part of any ecosystem, but it unsettles others, this inability to be satisfied. It is difficult—it is very difficult, to befriend where you wish to consume, to find those who, when they ask *Do I have you still*, when they end a letter with *Yours*, mean it in any substantive way.

So I go. I travel farther and faster and harder than most, and I read, and I write, and I love cities. To be alone in a crowd, apart and belonging, to have distance between what I see and what I am.

I am glad to know you love reading. Perhaps you should next write from a library—there's so much I want to recommend.

Best,

Blue

PS. Socrates! I wonder if we knew any of the same ones.

PPS. I kept knotting your name at night, but this salutation seemed wiser—I've learned to take warning from delight.

PPPS. Of course we're still going to win.

Blue is in a high place at night.

Wind blows. The air is cold, but she is not. Sharp rocks don't hurt her feet. Her job is to guard a growing thing, millennia in the making, a seed planted in the banked embers of the planet's heart that's riddled its slate surface with something like vines, sap, blood. Just beneath the surface, just waiting.

It will bloom soon.

Blue has fed it from time to time, as required. She has always known its purpose: a lion in waiting, a planet-size trap to spring, seeds planted long before prohibitive treaties about downthread interference. Blue is to watch it hatch, accomplish its purpose, then destroy its root system and leave no trace to be found or used by the other side. Garden has learned with the slow patience of green things how to prune enemy agents from the timeline, releasing ladybirds to their aphids, dragonflies to their mosquito larvae.

Blue is still thinking of larvae when she sees Red.

Time stops.

Blue carries nothing with her between strands except knowledge, purpose, tactics, and Red's letters. Memory is tipped and decanted into Garden, life to life to life, always deepening, thickening, growing new roots and efficiencies—but Red's letters she keeps in her own body, curled beneath her tongue like coins, printed in her fingers' tips, between the lines of her palms. She presses them against her teeth before kissing her marks, reads them over when she shifts her grip on motorcycle handles, dusts soldiers' chins with them in bar fights and barracks games. She thinks without thinking, often, of what she will name Red in her next letter—hides her lists in plausibly deniable dreamscapes, on the undersides of milkweed leaves, in shed chrysalis and wingtip. Vermillion Lie. Scarlet Tanager. Parthian Thread. My Red, Red Rose.

She looks at Red—thirteen, alone, vulnerable, so impossibly fragile and small—and a letter rises in her throat like bile.

I wanted to be seen.

She sees her and breaks like a wave.

She does not run the scenarios. She does not think, did Garden send me here to test me, does Garden know, does Garden want me to watch her die? She thinks nothing as the roots tense and twitch, as the planet blooms a mouth, a face, a body, a vastness rearing silent as owl flight in the perfect dark, a hunger with eyes and teeth, bred for silent, waiting years to scent one specific set of nanoscopic implants, to hatch and devour one bright red element of its surroundings. It looks a little like a lion, truth be told—mane of pale blue cilia, maw worthy of cinematic roars, though it will never make a sound—but for the size, the number of legs, the wings.

It steps out onto the cold, sharp ground. It sniffs the air, inclines its head in Red's direction.

Blue tears out its throat.

Her teeth are very sharp. She has four rows of them. Her double-banked eyes see beautifully in the dark. Her six legs end in tearing points, rip the voiceless creature into hot, pulsing meat. It gets its own in—good for the story she'll have to tell, she'll later think, when she can recover thought, when she can act again from something besides pure, obliterating need—and she bleeds in her wolf shape but makes no sound, nothing to distract Red from the absence of epiphany, the hollowing that left a space for another, the moment when she became Blue's.

Blue eats the carcass, all but its teeth and venom sack. That she tears carefully open on the rocks, tips a few drops into the hole it grew out of. The roots will lap it up, wither, and die; her story will be that the creature had soured, attacked her instead of its quarry. Enemy action, no doubt, having discovered the root system, made changes to it somewhere upthread.

An understandable but embarrassing mistake. Left Blue too injured to attempt her own correction, and at any rate there were the treaties—direct confrontation between agents so precariously downthread would be catastrophic for ambient Chaos levels.

The words fall into place like rain. Blue licks her bloodied snout, her paws, her gouged shoulder. She needs to do one more thing.

Slowly, keeping her wound out of sight, she walks where Red can see her. Keeping her distance, of course, and the words *padded past* in some dimness of mind. She does not look wounded; she is certain.

She looks at Red and sees tears on her face.

She stifles the urge to run—towards, or away. She carries her hunger like a compass rose (*stars rose—they are a rose, right?*), walks due south away from the north to which it points. Once she is out of sight, she tucks into a shallow cave and collapses, trembling, shifts her shape to human, finds her legs, her skin, the wound yawning larger and uglier than before, likely infected, needing care. She leans her back against the scalloped stone wall, closes her eyes, spreads her palms on the ground for extra support.

She puts one hand on a letter.

A letter to do Mrs. Leavitt proud: beautiful blue paper flecked with lavender buds and thistle petals, in a blue envelope with a red dollop of wax shutting it. There is no seal, no stamp—only red, red as the blood dripping from her shoulder.

She stares at it. Then she laughs, hollow and bare, and she sobs, and she clutches the letter against her heart and does not open it for a long time.

But she does. She reads it. Fever builds, sweat beads on her brow, but she reads it and reads it again and again and again.

Much later, the seeker comes. She finds the gutted creature's teeth. She plucks the two largest canines, fixes them into her mouth, and moves towards the cave.

There is nothing for her to find there except blood.

Dear Blue,

I—

I don't know what to say. Even perspicacious, almost prescient Mrs. Leavitt lacks a model. Birthdays, yes (it's mine, by the way, to the extent I have one); funerals, fine; on the occasion of a marriage, naturally. But she somehow neglects to frame a form for when your enemy saves—

Shit. I'm sorry. I can't keep up the joke. And it's wrong to call you enemy.

Thank you.

For saving me, obviously and for starters. I felt you climb down the braid. I am more sensitive to your footsteps, I think, than anyone alive. (And everyone is alive, somewhere in time. Even these digressions feel weak. I like them usually, my jokes. They feel like tacking in, not out, to the matter at hand. Less so now.) I followed you. I apologize for that, for trespassing on your privacy as you made yourself what you had to be to win.

I could not have beaten the beast alone. You're more ferocious than I am.

Do you look around in turn as you read these lines, seeking me? I'm gone, dear Blue, upthread, and you should be as well. We're neither of us safe here, and the longer you remain the less safe we become. You know the drill: Tremors spread from a traveler's foot, and though no other spider has grown so attuned to your tread as I have, the others aren't deaf. I'll have to see your eyes some other time. I leave you a letter, sealed in wax, a trace of perfume.

Scent, for me, is a medium. I rarely use it for ornamental purpose. I hope I've selected a fragrance to your taste. I asked the busboy in London Next for a sample of your tea a few letters back, brought it to a *parfumerie* in Phnom Penh (Strand 7922 C33 if you happen to like the smell; I'll enclose the address below), worked back and forth for a few years on the proper mix.

Anyway. Keep this. It's yours. It won't burn when you read the signature, it won't decay faster than any letter one woman in your beloved Strand 6 C19 would write to another. The paper's from Wuhan, Song dynasty, handmade: Leave it in a damp place and it will rot; mix it in water and you'll have a pulp. Destroy it on your own, in your own way, if you want. I won't mind. We all have our observers. And this letter is a knife at my neck, if cutting's what you want.

It's so hard to move, here, and reply to your last letter. I feel—I can't say precisely what. I'm shaken. You know the edges of old maps that promise monsters and mermaids? Here there be dragons?

I do not know what roads lead forward. But your letter hungers for reply.

I've read your last missive and reread it—in memory, as you warned me I would so long ago, preparing myself for a fall. I see you as a wave, as a bird, as a wolf. (My wolf, with the six legs and double-banked eyes.) I try not to think of you the same way twice. Thinking builds patterns in the brain, and those patterns can be read by one sufficiently determined, and Commandant, sometimes, is sufficiently determined—I think you'd like her. So I change your shape in my thoughts. It's amazing how much blue there is in the world, if you look. You're different colors of flame: Bismuth burns blue, and cerium, germanium, and arsenic. See? I pour you into things.

I suspect you see me plain by now—imagine me shifting, uncomfortable, exposed. My way was always the straightforward push, in one direction, without hesitation or restraint. I only worried you might view these long letters as the sign of a simple or a desperate mind. I worried—maybe you'll laugh—that you responded on sufferance.

So: Let me be clear.

I like writing you. I like reading you. When I finish your letters, I spend frantic hours in secret composing my replies, pondering ways to send them. I can trigger any combination of chemical ups and downs with a carefully worded phrase; a factory within me will smelt any drug I seek. But there's a rush in reading and sending against which no drug compares.

Speaking of exposed! If you have some grand plan, if the death your masters envisioned for my younger self was too quick and you'd rather see me disassembled for my parts, all you need do now is drop this letter where some other agent of my faction might find it. I could live with that. (Well, not for long, and painfully, but you take my meaning.)

So in this letter I am yours. Not Garden's, not your mission's, but yours, alone.

I am yours in other ways as well: yours as I watch the world for your signs, apophenic as a haruspex; yours as I debate methods, motives, chances of delivery; yours as I review your words by their sequence, their sound, smell, taste, taking care no one memory of them becomes too worn. Yours. Still, I suspect you will appreciate the token.

I'll try for a library next time. I hope you understand my need for a change of plans.

Yours,

Red

Red runs the table, to stop herself from thinking.

In Strand 622 C19 Beijing, she, uncomfortable in her sheathing of silk (but channeling Blue), starts a debate about canal construction that feeds into a debate about public morality that spurs a principled, incorruptible bureaucrat named Lin to accept an Imperial dare. If Lin clears drug-smuggling foreigners from Guangzhou, he will have funding for his infrastructure project. When Lin reaches Guangzhou and tries to break the drug trade, a war begins, and Red slips away.

In fourteenth-century Axum, Islamicized and strong in Strand 3329, Red, in shadows, stabs a man who's about to stab another man who's wandering home buzzed on espresso, sugar, and math. The man Red stabs dies. The mathematician wakes up the next day and invents a form of thought that, in another strand, much later, will be called hyperbolic geometry. Red's already gone.

In ninth century al-Andalus she serves the right tea, at the right time. In the diamond city of Zanj she strangles a man with a silken cord. She seeds the Strand 9 Amazon Basin with defanged versions of European superbugs ten centuries before first contact, and when conquistadors arrive, they face locals by the millions, strong, thriving communities that won't perish by mere contact with the world across the waves. She kills again and again, frequently, but not always, to save.

And she watches over her shoulder.

A shadow follows her. She has no proof, but she knows, as bones know their breaking stress.

Commandant must suspect. A drop in her efficiencies would point to compromise. So Red throws herself into her tasks: works riskier assignments than Commandant would ever require, succeeds beautifully, brutally. Time and again, empty, she wins.

She climbs upthread and down; she braids and unbraids history's hair.

Red rarely sleeps, but when she does, she lies still, eyes closed in the dark, and lets herself see lapis, taste iris petals and ice, hear a blue jay's shriek. She collects blues and keeps them.

When she is sure no one is watching, she rereads the letters she's carved into herself.

All this running and murder merely passes time. She waits and waits. For the guillotine: She's been trapped, the one for whom she waits has fed Commandant the letter she left behind, and Commandant's just playing her out now, squeezing Red for work until the Chaos Oracle indicates she has marginally more value crushed.

My dear Cochineal—

Or: Blue (she lets herself think that name once in a two-mooned month) read her letter and recoiled. Red wrote too much too fast. Her pen had a heart inside, and the nib was a wound in a vein. She stained the page with herself. She sometimes forgets what she wrote, save that it was true, and the writing hurt. But butterfly wings break when touched. Red knows her own weaknesses as well as anyone. She presses too hard, breaks what she would embrace, tears what she would touch to her teeth.

She dreams of a morpho butterfly with wings spread large as a world.

She strangles, screws, builds. She works.

She watches birds.

There are so damn many birds. She never heeded them before; knowledge of them (whose call is that, which is male and which female, what's the name of the duck with the emerald head) is all stored on the index, but when has she needed it? She planned to get to it one day; she plans to get to everything one day.

But now she learns the names from books. She pulls some

from the index to save time and because books are heavy, but she does not leave the knowledge in the cloud. She repeats the names to herself; she carves patterns into her eyes.

She burns three astronauts in their cockpit on a launchpad. Every cause needs sacrifices. The stench of seared pork and sour rubber catches in her lungs, and she flees upthread, lets no one see her weep. Collapses on the bank of the Ohio River, bends double, vomits in a bush, crawls away, and cries out the rubber and the screams. She strips. She wades into the water until it covers her head. A flock of Canada geese dawn north and paint the sky green-black with the creaks of their wings.

She stops the air bubbling from her mouth.

The geese settle on the river. Their legs churn the water. They stay half an hour, only to lift off in a thunderclap of feathers.

She emerges.

One goose waits on the shore, for her.

She kneels.

It lays its head on her shoulder.

Then it leaves, and two feathers remain.

Red clutches them to her for a long time before she reads.

Later, farther south, a great horned owl takes the goose, and the seeker, weeping, eats its heart.

When Red enters the clearing, only footprints and the cored goose remain.

My dear Miskowaanzhe,

I write to you in the dark before dawn, slowly, long-hand, chalk on slate—later I will translate these words into feathers. There is a small hill from which I can watch the sun set over the Outaouais River; every evening I see a red sky bleed over blue water and think of us. Have you ever watched this kind of sunset? The colours don't blend: the redder the sky the bluer the water, as we tilt away from the sun.

I'm embedded, now, in a strand beloved of Garden—one of the ones where this continent wasn't critically overrun by settlers with philosophies and modes of production inimical to our Shift—on a research mission, tugging at and wicking fibres for easier braiding into other strands. Always a balancing act, of course, to give without losing, to support without weakening. Everything a weaving.

I've been placed here to convalesce, I think. Garden doesn't always spell these things out but does know my fondness for hummingbirds and migrating geese. I'm grateful. It is good to write with leisure. I hope, while here, to stretch my letters out, if only because they will have to find you at a lived pace—it will be a long while before I walk the braid again.

I'm married and will soon wake my husband with rose-hip tea and breakfast before sending him out to train. He's a good man, a runner and a scout, and the days are getting cooler, so there are a great many messages and supplies to send and share before the storytelling season sets in and blankets us indoors.

It is such luxury to dwell in these details—to share them with you. I want, Red—I want to give you things.

Have you ever tasted rose hips, in tea or jam? A tart sourness that cleans the teeth, refreshes, smells like a good morning. A mash of rose hips and mint keeps me steepling my fingers all day long, to keep those scents in my head. Sumac, too—I think you might like sumac.

I find myself naming red things that aren't sweet.

Your letter—your last letter. Be certain that I won't drop it where any of your fellows can read it. It's mine. I am careful with what belongs to me.

Few things do, you know—belong to me. In Garden we belong to one another in a way that obliterates the term. We sink and swell and bud and bloom together; we infuse Garden; Garden spreads through us. But Garden dislikes words. Words are abstraction, break off from the green; words are patterns in the way fences and trenches are. Words hurt. I can hide in words so long as I scatter them through my body; to read your letters is to gather flowers from within myself, pluck a blossom here, a fern there, arrange and rearrange them in ways to suit a sunny room.

It amuses me to think of liking your Commandant. What a strange Strand that would be.

I keep turning away from speaking of your letter. I feel—to speak of it would be to contain what it did to me, to make it small. I don't want to do that. I suppose in some ways I'm more Garden's child than she knows. Even poetry, which breaks language into meaning—poetry ossifies, in time, the way trees do. What's supple, whipping, soft, and fresh grows hard, grows armor. If I could touch you, put my finger to your temple and sink you into me the way Garden does—perhaps then. But I would never.

So this letter instead.

I ramble, it seems, when writing to the darkness by hand. How embarrassing. I'm quite certain I've never rambled a day in my life before this. Another thing to give you: this first, for me.

Yours,

Blue

PS. Should this find you near a library, I recommend *Travel Light* by Naomi Mitchison. It's the same in all strands in which it exists. It might be a comfort to you on the move—I can tell you're moving a lot right now.
PPS. Thank you. For the letter.

Blue walks in the hush-light before dawn and looks for a sign.

Her work here is slow but never boring; one of Blue's virtues as an operative is the thoroughness she brings to every life. Her husband will be important to the daughter of a rival's friend, and the conversations Blue has with him, the gifts she makes him, the dreams towards which she rocks him in their bed will spiral tendrils of possibility from this strand into others, send tremors to shift and shake the future's boughs in Garden's direction.

It is a gift from Garden that her role here requires such thorough, deliberate in-dwelling; that to wander in the woods and think of birds and trees and colours is expected of her, is mission critical. Blue loves cities—their anonymity, their smells and sounds—but she loves forests, too, places other people call quiet that are anything but. Blue listens to jays, woodpeckers, grackles, laughs at hummingbirds jousting on the wing. She holds out her hands for nuthatches and chickadees, black-and-white warblers, and they flit to her, make branches of her fingers. She strokes sapsuckers' crests without naming the colour, makes a needle and a thread of the thrill she feels in touching it, then stitches it into the joy Garden expects her to feel in the woods.

There's a scar on her shoulder in every shape now, a puckered tracery of trauma. Wolves shy from her, love her from a distance.

Because she is expected to amble in this way, it's relatively easy to disguise her searching; because she has been turning the last season's leaves, picking up crow skulls, the shed and drying velvet of antlers, foxes' teeth, it is not at all noteworthy that she goes still as prey in the presence of a great grey owl, its wizard face inclined to her, the sheen of its feathers ruffling a colour like the retreating night.

It stands, serene and dignified, in the hollow of an oak and looks at her.

Then it horks up a sizeable pellet, ruffles itself, and flies away.

Blue laughs—sudden, sharp—and stoops to pocket the pellet. She turns it over in the fingers of one hand without looking at it, just another curio for her collection. She does not take her hand off it until she is back home; she waits until sunset, when she can be looking at the scarletting sky as she cuts carefully into the pellet and finds something there to read.

Years later, a seeker scours the area just shy of the speed of sound, blurs in and out of sight, and carries tiny fragments of bone back into the braid.

Dearest Lapis,

Yes! I've been moving. They have us—well, me, really—all over these days, upthread and down, new assignments gathering by the minute. Your side's tricks and traps took their toll, so our missions multiply to make up the difference. But enough of the war. Enough to say: I write at haste.

I was about to ask you to forgive my brevity. As I went to write that, though, I saw you shaking your head. You were right, back when—I have built a you within me, or you have. I wonder what of me there is in you.

Thank you for your letter, more than I can say. It found me in a moment of hunger.

Words can wound—but they're bridges, too. (Like the bridges that are all that Genghis left behind.) Though maybe a bridge can also be a wound? To paraphrase a prophet: Letters are structures, not events. Yours give me a place to live inside.

My memories of you spread through millennia,

and each highlights you in motion. This picture of you at home, with husband, with rose-hip tea, with sunset and river, swells my heart. A stippling of sea skin indicates the whale beneath—or dots of star shape a bear light-years big—so I trace your life now, from these hints. I imagine you waking, sleeping, watching geese, working hard outside, with arms and back and legs and period technology. I will find some sumac when next I'm where it grows. I confess I'm only familiar with the poison variety, which I don't think you mean.

Perhaps someday they'll assign us side by side, in some small village far upthread, deep cover, each watching each, and we can make tea together, trade books, report home sanitized accounts of each other's doings. I think I'd still write letters, even then.

Read the Mitchison. Loved it. (Though that seems too quick a summary—I get what you mean about words, now.) It hit me. Especially the dragons and Odin and the ending. I had a harder time with the Constantinople section—I may be missing some context there, though I can see what place it holds in the book, and the trickery reminds me of pieces of *Don Quixote*. But the final revelation—about the kings and the dragons—yes.

Funny how we always think of knights as fighting dragons, when in fact they work for them.

Garden seems to like roots, and this book roots in rootlessness. Are you a tumbleweed, then? A dandelion seed?

You are yourself, and so remain, as I remain,

Yours,

Red

PS. Owls are fascinating creatures, but it's harder than I'd thought to convince them to take food. Maybe this one didn't trust me.

PPS. I don't mean to unnerve you, but—are you seeing shadows? I may have picked one up. No proof yet, and I may well be paranoid, but paranoia doesn't mean I'm wrong. Commandant hasn't let on she suspects anything, at least not yet. Take care.

PPPS. Really. That book. In a moment of daring I commended it to the attention of a few major critics in Strand 623; hard to generate momentum, but you never know—new strands rise all the time. Send me more.

Red wins a battle between starfleets in the far future of Strand 2218. As the great *Gallumfry* lists planetward, raining escape pods, as battle stations wilt like flowers tossed into flame, as radio bands crackle triumph and swiftskimmers swoop after fleeing voidtails, as guns speak their last arguments into mute space, she slips away. The triumph feels stale and swift. She used to love such fire. Now it only reminds her of who's not there.

She climbs upthread, taking solace in the past.

Red rarely seeks company with others of her kind. They are oddballs all—decanted after being found, at some point in their development, deviant. Or, the most deviant of all, those who decanted themselves. They are not at peace and play in the celestial rose. They carve their bodies off, they introduce asymmetry.

They would make this war, she thinks, *if there were not a war already made for them to make.*

But she seeks company now, in one of the places she can always find it.

Sun hammers the streets of Rome. A man with a lean face and a sharp nose and a laurel crown walks, attended, past the Theater of Pompey. Others intercept him, summon him inside. A crowd's waiting there, in the shadows: the senators, their servants, and others.

"Have you," Red asks one of the others, "ever felt you're being followed? That Commandant is spying on you?"

One senator offers Caesar a petition.

"Followed?" says the man with the broken nose to her left. "By the enemy, sometimes. By the Agency? If Commandant wanted to spy on us, she could read our minds."

Caesar waves off the petition, but the senators cluster close.

"Someone's dogged my tracks," Red says. "But they're gone as soon as I think to catch them."

"Enemy agent," says the woman to her right.

"These are jaunts of my own, research trips, not counterplay. How would an enemy agent know where I was going?"

One senator draws a knife. He tries to stab Caesar in the back, but Caesar catches his hand.

"If it is Commandant," says the man with the broken nose, "why worry?"

She frowns. "I would like to know if my loyalty is being tested."

The man whose hand has been caught shouts for help in Greek. Knives slither from senators' sheathes.

"That would defeat the purpose of the test," observes the woman. "Come on. We'll miss the fun." She has a wide grin and a long blade.

Caesar shouts some words, but they're lost in the din as the killers descend. Red shrugs and sighs and joins them. Their war holds few enough chances to cut loose, and she can't be seen to pass them up. Blood sticks to her hands. She washes them later, in another river, far away.

Leaves are turning in the Ohio woods when the geese land. One departs from the flock to approach. Red ponders the fate of the last goose to bring her a letter and feels a moment's guilt.

Twine loops the goose's neck, and from the twine hangs a pouch of thin leather.

Her hands tremble as she opens the pouch. Six seeds lie inside, tiny crimson teardrops with tinier numbers scratched into their surface, one through six. On the leather, in an ink too blue for this continent or strand, handwriting she knows well, though she's only seen it once, traces *Do you trust me?*

She sits in the woods, alone.

She does.

Red trusts her so far down in the bone she has to ponder a long while to realize what distrust might imply—what these seeds might be, what they might do to her if she's wrong.

She eats the first three seeds one by one. She should be sitting beneath a baobab tree, but she slumps under a buckeye instead, surrounded by spiked shells.

As each letter unfolds inside her mind, she frames it in the palace of her memory. She webs words to cobalt and lapis, she weds them to the robes of Mary in San Marco frescoes, to paint on porcelain, to the color inside a glacier crack. She will not let her go.

The third seed, with its third letter, drops Red into a swoon.

She wakes at a rustle of buckeye shells to find the last three seeds still clutched in her fist, but the leather bag missing. She hears footsteps in the wood and pursues them: A shadow darts before her, always out of reach, and then it's gone, and she falls panting to her knees in the empty wood.

Dear Price Greater Than Rubies,

I have been needle-felting for my lover's sister's children: an owlet for one, a fawn for the other. Curious to use so delicate a tool for such savage work—you take a needle so fine you wouldn't feel it in your flesh, then stab it through a mess of roving over and over until the fibres settle into shape.

I feel you, the needle of you, dancing up and downthread with breathtaking abandon. I feel your hand in places I've touched. You move so fast, so furious, and in your wake the braid thickens, admits fewer and fewer strands, while Garden scowls thunderclaps and bids me deepen my work.

I like to think of all the ways I could have stopped you, were I so inclined.

Sometimes I am inclined. Sometimes I sit here stationary, and know you so swift and sure, and think, *I must prove myself her equal again*—and the sharp, electric ache to stop you just to see you admire me is a kind of needle too.

I have six months to fill before I can send this to

you, so I am writing in pieces—parcelling out the words I wish you to have, though you'll of course read them all at once. Or perhaps you won't? Perhaps you'll want to save these seeds to absorb at your leisure, perhaps even at the pace of my writing them. But why waste so much time? More dangerous to keep them on you, where they can be found. Better to read them all at once.

At any rate, this is staghorn sumac: not poisonous, delicious mixed into meats, salads, tobacco. Taste how tart it is, how tangy; grind it into a spice to sprinkle or smoke, or soak the berry heads whole and get something like lemonade.

These seeds, for you, are best eaten one at a time, rolled around your tongue and broken beneath your teeth.

Yours,

Blue

PS. I love writing in aftertaste.
PPS. I hope you noticed the difference between this sumac and the poisonous one. Only one of them is red.

• • •

My dear Sugar Maple,

We're tapping the trees, boiling sap down for syrup and hard candy. I like you to know, with my words in your mouth, the places and ways in which I think of you. It feels good to be reciprocal; eat this part of me while I drive reeds into the depth of you, spill out something sweet.

I wish sometimes I could be less fierce with you. No—I feel sometimes like I ought to want to be less fierce with you. That this—whatever this is—would be better served by tenderness, by gentle kindness. Instead I write of spilling out your sap-guts with reeds. I hope you can forgive this. To be soft, for me, is so often pretense, and pretense does not come easily while writing to you.

You wrote of being in a village upthread together, living as friends and neighbours do, and I could have swallowed this valley whole and still not have sated my hunger for the thought. Instead I wick the longing into thread, pass it through your needle eye, and sew it into hiding somewhere beneath my skin, embroider my next letter to you one stitch at a time.

Yours,

Blue

• • •

Dear Sailor's Delight,

The snow's gone and everything is warming, as if the sun were knuckling into the earth with both hands and kneading it into release. Planting time on the horizon—and I take this phrase and turn it over, smile at how Garden seeds time, makes time a planting more subtle than desert seasons, and the horizon is a promise.

I have waited until now to address your concern about shadows. I have paid careful attention. There was a time, earlier in our correspondence, when I was absolutely certain of being trailed— little things, faint, difficult to name, but you know the feeling of walking into a room where someone has recently been and left? Like that, but in reverse. Never followed, quite, but . . . trailed.

But I've not felt this since being embedded, which may be cause for concern. When Garden embeds an agent—as I'm sure your Commandant has noticed—they are near impossible to approach, indistinguishable from their surroundings, so thoroughly enmeshed in the fabric of strands that to cut us out would tear unsightly holes through which Chaos pours, Chaos no one downthread wants, not even your Oracle, who lives and breathes the stuff. Too unpredictable, too difficult to manage, the cost/benefit all askew—so you catch us on the move, in between, while we're dancing the braid as well, touching lives only lightly. Even Garden has difficulty reaching us with the more nuanced branches of their consciousness; to be an agent out of time and approach someone embedded you'd need to practically wear their skin before the braid would allow you within fifty years or a thousand miles of their position.

You'll ask, *But how are you able to send me letters in the contents of birds' stomachs?* Think of birds as a comms channel I can open and close seasonally; fellow operatives relate their work to me at the equinoxes; Garden blooms more brightly in my belly. There's enough traffic that it's a simple matter to disguise incoming and out-going correspondence, misdirect, hide in plain sight. Enemy agents, though—I've heard stories of what happens to those of your side who try to push through to one of our plantings. Imagine walking through a thorn hedge that grows thicker, harder, sharper the more you push into it, and you'll have something of what it's like—but for acres, for decades, until you're ribboned and rent into tinsel.

All this to say, I'm not being followed; if you are, I'll send out what feelers I can to see if it's my people. It may well be—Garden's clearly been interested in you since you were small. But I've every confidence in your ability to evade and out-maneuver anyone from my side.

Anyone who isn't me.

If it's your people, that's more complicated and troubling. Be careful.

Yours,

Blue

PS. Any information you can give me about the quality of shadow—a scent, a qualifying colour of feeling, the nightmare you woke from after you thought yourself safe—will help me investigate. Though I suppose I never did learn if you dream.

Blue is braiding grasses between her fingers.

It looks like purest idleness: a long-haired woman at day's end, painted in sunset, cross-legged near the river, weaving for pleasure. She is not making baskets or nets, not even crowns or garlands for the children running barefoot nearby.

What she does is study. What she does is play, in six dimensions, a game of chess in which every piece is a game of Go, whole boards of black and white stones dancing around each other, pushed, knights turned rooks, iterations of atari carefully constructing checkmate. She lays grass over grass over grass and studies, not only the geometries of green, but the calculus of scent and heat, the thermodynamics of understory, the velocity of birdsong.

While so enmeshed—knotting grass to grackle scold, the smell of leaf mold to sun's azimuth—a tree swallow swoops near, scissors her peripheral vision, severs her from trancing reverie with its dissonance. It flashes blue at her eyes' edge, stuns her with its unaccountable presence. There are tree swallows aplenty, but this one is wrong: This one approaches an empty nest in autumn, a nest that she was near to harvesting to show her nephew and teach him about how much weaving can be learned from birds.

She stands, and the grasses fall from her hand like seeds. She follows the swallow, watches as it deposits a damselfly in the nest and flies away.

She climbs, plucks the insect from the muddy twigs, hops back down. In the damsel's needle-body, checkered in black and blue, she reads a letter.

She looks from the dead damsel to the scattering it's made of her thoughts, fistfuls of green and gold heaped uselessly together, and feels nothing but a knifing, knotting happiness as she opens her mouth to devour it, wings and all.

Years later, a seeker shadows the grass where Blue lay. She scoops up a handful, then melts away.

My Blueprint,

I have read your first three sumac letters. I cannot let them go unanswered, though I fear to write without knowing what comes next. (I taste the letters still. They linger. They undermine all other flavors, pipe them full of you.) Perhaps I'll ask a question answered later. Perhaps I'll write a sentence that offends.

But if you hunger, I swell. You have me watching birds, and though I don't know their names like you know them, I have seen small bright singers puff before they trill. That's how I feel. I sing myself out to you, and my talons clutch the branch, and I am wrung out until your next letter gives me breath, fills me to bursting.

I miss you in the field. I miss defeat. I miss the chase, the fury. I miss victories well earned. Your fellows have their intrigues and their passions, and now and again a clever play, but there's none so intricate, so careful, so assured. You've whetted me like a stone. I feel almost invincible in our battles' wake: a kind of Achilles, fleet footed and light of touch. Only in this nonexistent place our letters weave do I feel weak.

How I love to have no armor here.

You wish you could hold me at knifepoint again. You do, still, in a way. So long as I bear these last three seeds in a hollow behind my eye, you are a blade against my back. I love the danger of it. Besides, I am not so naive as to think your posting to this strand entirely lacks purpose. Your Garden works slowly, works through lives. It burrows you deep, and through you wreaks great change, while we strive upon the surface.

And in your absence you are deadly as a blade. Lacking letters, lacking the tremors of your foot-steps through time, I seek out your memories; I ask myself what you would say and do if you were here. I imagine you reaching over my shoulder to correct my hand on a victim's throat, to guide the braiding of a strand.

I am being watched. The shadow, my Seeker, steals after me. I glimpse it in the purplish gloam-ing, but where I chase it, it is not. Smells: hard to say, though hints of ozone and burnt maple. It takes many forms. I worry it is just a phantom, a consequence of my breaking mind. I had hoped to catch it, kill it, prove myself sane (or not) before consuming your next letters. I cannot endanger us, endanger you, any further. But I am the songbird running out of air, and I must breathe.

I dream.

They've freed us from sleep as from hunger. But I like exhaustion, call it a kink or what you will, and in my work upthread it's often convenient to impersonate humanity. So I tire myself with work, and I sleep, and dreams come.

I dream of you. I keep more of you inside my mind, my physical, personal, squishy mind, than I keep of any other world or time. I dream myself a seed between your teeth, or a tree tapped by your reed. I dream of thorns and gardens, and I dream of tea.

The work waits. They'll catch me here if I remain. More soon, after I've put this shadow to bed, after we're safe.

Yours,

Red

Red's off to catch a shadow.

She lays traps. She doubles back in time to build dead ends of history; she tangles strands. Her quarry, whose quarry she is in turn, slips free, leaving now a sound, now a taste on the air, nothing so grand as a thread caught on a thorn.

In downthread server farms couched in remnant icebergs' hearts, she circles back upon her trail, glimpses the shadow, fires her fléchette pistol through rackspace gaps, birthing blue sparks.

In Asoka's court, an acrobat, she climbs, flips, turns, sifting a thousand-person crowd for a single predator, one watcher who should not be there. She smells the shadow, and smells it slip away.

She storms the falling walls of Jericho, and in dense streets she hears a footstep on stone that does not belong. She turns, draws, lets fly. An arrow embeds itself in stone.

She races gravcycles through a crystal forest coursing with the brilliant pulse of human beings whose physical bodies have been rendered, like bacon fat, until the fragrance of their minds expands to fill all space. Whatever she is seeking, whatever's seeking her, it does not catch her there, though she does not catch it in return.

She finds a pregnant possibility by a riverbed and waits. She does not know why she thinks the shadow will visit here, but she feels she's growing to know the thing, its habits, when it visits her and when it keeps away. She seeds the air with nanobots, weaves servants through the grass; she sets drone spies and sentry cameras; she tasks a satellite to her service. She watches the river, cautious, quiet, for seven months. She blinks once, and when she opens her eyes, she feels the moment has passed: The shadow has been and gone, and she's learned nothing. No traps have sprung, the nanobots failed to register a presence, the cameras have one by one turned off, and the satellite orbits mute and broken.

Red aches for the letters she keeps behind her eye.

She cannot breathe. A great hand clutches her about the chest, squeezing. She feels trapped in her skin, bound beneath her skull. Dreams help, and memories, but dreams and memories are not enough. She wants to imagine a laugh. She must wait. She cannot wait.

Far, far upthread, she sits beneath something like a

willow tree in a dinosaur swamp, holds a sumac seed between her teeth, and bites.

Red sits still for hours. Night falls. Wind rustles ferns. An apatosaur lumbers past, ruffling its feathers.

She lets herself feel. The organs that buffer her emotions from physical response shut down, and all she's hidden washes over her. Her heart quakes. She heaves in gulps of breath, and she is so alone.

A hand settles on her shoulder.

She catches the shadow's wrist.

The shadow throws her, and she throws it in turn. They tumble through undergrowth; they crash against an enormous mushroom's trunk. Small lizards scuttle out. The shadow's afoot, but Red snares its leg in hers, brings it down. She goes for the joint lock, but her own leg's locked in turn. She wriggles free, punches three, four times, each one blocked easily. Implants burn. Wings part from her back to vent waste heat; she hits hard. She catches the shadow in the ribs, but those bones do not break. The shadow floats behind her, touches her shoulder, and her arm goes limp. Red throws her weight back, snares its arm as she falls. They slip together in the mud. Red's fingers hook to claws. She tries to find a throat. Finds it. Clutches.

And somehow the shadow slips free and leaves her lying, panting, furious, alone in the mud.

She curses the stars that watch the dinosaur night.

Red can bear the wait no longer.

She rises, staggers to a river, washes her hands. Pops out her left eye with her thumb and probes the socket until she finds the three sumac seeds. (The one she ate earlier was a fake.)

Fuck safety. Fuck the shadow.

Red knows hunger now.

She eats the first seed beneath the canopy.

She chokes. She curls around herself. She cannot breathe. She crumbles around her heart.

The organs, she remembers, are turned off. This pain is new.

She does not turn them on again before she eats the second seed.

Out in the swamp, great beasts echo her groan. She is not a person anymore. She is a toad; she is a rabbit in the hunter's hand; she is a fish. She is, briefly, Blue, alone with Red, and together.

She eats the third letter.

Silence claims the swamp.

The aftertaste stings her tongue and fills her. She weeps, and laughs into her tears, and lets herself fall. They might find her, kill her, here. She does not care.

Among the dinosaurs, Red sleeps.

Seeker, muddy, battered, torn, finds her sleeping, touches her tears with an ungloved hand, and tastes them before she goes.

Dear Strawberry,

Summer settles like a bee on clover—golden, busy, here then gone. There's so much to do. I love this part of being embedded, love feeling thoroughly wrung out at day's end: no recuperation ponds, no healing sap, no quiet green murmuring in my marrow—just sweat and salt and sun on my back, everyone loving their bodies while knowing their bodies, this beautiful dance.

We pick berries. We fish the rivers. We hunt ducks and geese. We tend the gardens. We organize festivals, light fires, discuss philosophy, fight skirmishes where necessary. People die; people live. I have been laughing a great deal, this summer, and it has been so easy.

You say my letter found you in a moment of hunger. How to say what it means to me, that I might have taught you this—shared it, somehow, infected you with it. I hope it isn't a burden at the same time that I want you seared by it. I want to sharpen your hungers fully as much as I long to satisfy them, one letter-seed at a time.

I want to tell you something about myself. Something true, or nothing at all.

Yours,

Blue

PS. I'm so happy you read the Mitchison. Constantinople is difficult—but it helps sometimes to think of the book as moving through phases of storytelling time. Myth and legend give way to history, which gives way again to myth, like curtains parting and meeting again on either side of a performance. Halla begins in Mitchison's Norse myths outside of book-time, and by the end has been absorbed—embedded, perhaps—into the myths of those she travelled with. All good stories travel from the outside in.

• • •

Dear Raspberry,

It's not that I never noticed before how many red things there are in the world. It's that they were never any more relevant to me than green or white or gold. Now it's as if the whole world sings to me in petals, feathers, pebbles, blood. Not that it didn't before—Garden loves music with a depth impossible to sound—but now its song's for me alone.

Alone. I want to tell you about when I learned that word, really, with all of me. The reason I'm a tumbleweed, a dandelion seed, a stone rolling until she's planted in place, then kicked up again.

We're grown, I think you know—seeds planted, roots combing through time, until Garden repots us in different soil. Our seeding points are so thoroughly embedded that what I mentioned before about approach is inconceivable: Garden goes to seed, blows us away, and we burrow into the braidedness of time and mesh with it. There is no scouring hedge to pass through; we are the hedge, entirely, rosebuds with thorns for petals. The only way to access us is to enter Garden so far downthread that most of our own agents can't manage it, find the umbilical taproot that links us to Garden, and then navigate it upthread like salmon in a stream. Which, if any of you could do, would mean we were vanquished already—if you had that kind of access to Garden, you could raze our whole Shift.

(I can't—I shouldn't tell you this. In spite of all, I keep thinking—this could be such a long con, this could be the information you wanted all along, this—but does it matter, really? The point of no return was millennia from now, kept folded up small and tea scented in a subcutaneous sack I grew beneath my left thigh. Not exactly a locket full of hair, but no reason that should be less grotesque to the disembodied, I suppose.)

Anyway.

I never mentioned, I think, the strand in which Garden planted the seed of me—"to begin my life with the beginning of my life" feels absurd to such as us, doesn't it?—but it wasn't anything special; Strand 141's Albic parts, in the same year as the death of its Chatterton, though I beg you not to cast my horoscope. When I was very small, still just barely a sprout of Garden rooted through a five-year-old girl, I got sick. This wasn't unusual—we're often deliberately made sick, inoculated against far-future diseases, dosed with varying degrees of immortality, whatever it takes to make us into what we need to be when Garden releases us into the wholeness of the braid.

But this was different. This wasn't Garden

infecting me to strengthen me; this was someone infecting me to get at Garden.

This should have been impossible. I was enmeshed. But something, somehow—I was compromised by enemy action. It has the quality of fairy tale to me; I was sleepy, in that space between dream and waking when one can't be certain whether what one's seeing is real or a storm of nanites rewiring your synapses.

(I had to deal with that once. It was unpleasant. I hope you never have to electrocute yourself to burn bugs out of your brain. Then again maybe that's covered in basic training for your lot.)

I remember a kiss and something to eat. It was so kind, I couldn't fathom it as unfriendly. As fairy tale as it gets, really. I remember bright light, and then— hunger. Hunger that was turning me inside out, hunger in the most primal way imaginable, hunger that obliterated every other thing—I couldn't see, I was so hungry, I couldn't breathe, and it was like something was opening up inside me and telling me to *seek*. I think some part of me must have been screaming, but I couldn't tell you which; my body was an alarm bell sounding. I turned all of myself toward Garden to be fed, to stem this, to stop me from disappearing—

And Garden cut me off.

Which is standard operating procedure. Garden must endure. Garden can, does, has, will shed pieces, always, cuttings, flowers, fruit, but Garden endures and grows stronger again. Garden couldn't let the hunger reach beyond me.

I understand that now, but at the time . . . I had never been alone. And I think of you, making that aloneness for yourself apart from the others as a choice—but for me, I was only my own body, only my own senses, only a girl whose parents were running to her because she had a bad dream. I touched their faces, and they were mine; I touched the bed I was on, smelled apples stewing somewhere outside. It was as if, in my own small way, I'd become Garden—so me in my wholeness, me in my fingers, in my hair, in my skin, whole the way Garden is whole, but apart.

The hunger simmered in me for a week, during which I ate so much my parents whispered of egg-shell stews and hot pokers. I learned to hide it. And then, after a year, Garden took me back.

Grafted me back on as if we'd never severed, probed and peered and sorted through me, doused me in medicines and protection, scoured me inside and out. Nothing was found. My maturation had been sped up oddly, perhaps, but that was all. And after some keen scrutiny during the next few years, the fears that I'd been compromised were mostly laid to rest; nothing in the braid suggested corruption beginning from my strand. Important, too, to broadcast that the attempt at penetrating enmeshment had been unsuccessful (though it had succeeded—but as they never tried it again, Garden's gambit there must have convinced the relevant parties). So Garden deployed me, made much of me, praised and elevated me, but always at something like arm's length.

My eccentricities are tolerated: my love of cities, of poetry, my appreciation for being rootless, for being, in some ways, more Gardener than Garden, or Gardened. My appetites, that being flooded with Garden can't seem to sate.

You, though, Red—

. . .

My Apple Tree, my Brightness,

Sometimes when you write, you say things I stopped myself from saying. I wanted to say, *I want to make you tea to drink*, but didn't, and you wrote to me of doing so; I wanted to say, *your letter lives inside me in the most literal way possible*, but didn't, and you wrote to me of structures and events. I wanted to say, *words hurt, but metaphors go between, like bridges, and words are like stone to build bridges, hewn from the earth in agony but making a new thing, a shared thing, a thing that is more than one Shift*.

But I didn't, and you spoke of wounds.

I want to say, now, before you can beat me to it—Red, when I think of this seed in your mouth I imagine having placed it there myself, my fingers on your lips.

I don't know what this means. This feels like being cut off, again, in the strangest way—feels like teetering on the brink of something that will unmake me.

But I trust you.

Take these years of mine, take these seeds, and let them grow me something similar in reply? I miss the length of your letters.

Love,

Blue

Even very long engagements come to an end.

It happens like this: Blue, belly on the ground, ankles in the air, elbows and forearms printed with twigs and stems, tangles grasses.

The game board that is a sphere and a braid and a forest of pleached trees encompasses her and the grasses. Garden asserts, over and again, that their rival Shift relies too much on tricking time, evading it, skimming across it like stones, dipping in distasteful toes, thinking to divert its currents by rippling its surface. You must dwell, says Garden, within time to shift it in lasting ways; play a slow game, but win.

Blue's focus stills everything around her. She floods herself with green, follows networks of roots through earth and air and water while building her braid.

Then she stops. Her hand trembles.

I imagine you reaching over my shoulder to correct my

hand on a victim's throat, to guide the braiding of a strand.

She'd never noticed her hands before—her own hand as a strand.

It changes everything. The grasses knot perfectly. The world tips sideways as she runs, as multidimensional millennia resolve into a perfect Go board with an impossible last liberty just waiting for Garden to rise up through and claim, choking the Agency like a banyan strangles its host.

The deep work swells within her as she coheres with Garden, as she feels Garden jubilate like a river in spring, as Garden floods her with love and approval enough to sate a century of orphans.

It's almost enough. It's unlike anything Garden has ever given her since that first severing. But within the swirling glow of cool, soothing colours she keeps a tiny vein of herself apart: sees a hand on a hand on a throat and thinks, *I can't wait for Red to see.*

Dear Blue,

I wish I could see your triumph. Knowing something of your mission, of the nature of your embedment, having committed the beat of your footsteps to my heart, I sense the change you will wreak upon us. The season turns. You will be free—from your recovery and from your task. I'll be sent, no doubt, to undo the damage you've caused. And we'll run again, the two of us, upthread and down, firefighter and fire starter, two predators only sated by each other's words.

Do you laugh, sea foam? Do you smile, ice, and observe your triumph with an angel's remove? Sapphire-flamed phoenix, risen, do you command me once again to look upon your works and despair?

I distract myself. I talk of tactics and of methods. I say how I know how I know. I make metaphors to approach the enormous fact of you on slant.

I send you this letter on a falling star. Reentry will score and test it but will not melt it away. I write in fire across the sky, a plummet to match your rise.

Your praise cuts me, because though I speak so easily of certain things, though I rush through ground that to you seems mined, it's only earth to me. But your last letter . . . I am so good at missing things. At making myself not see. I stand at a cliff's edge, and—hell.

I love you, Blue.

Have I always? Haven't I?

When did it happen? Or has it always happened? Like your victory, love spreads back through time. It claims our earliest association, our battles and losses. Assassinations become assignations. There was, I am sure, a time I did not know you. Or did I dream that me, as I've so often dreamed of you? Have we always fulfilled one another in the chase? I remember hunting you through Samarkand, thrilling to think I might touch the loosening strands of your hair.

I want to be a body for you.

I want to chase you, find you, I want to be eluded and teased and adored; I want to be defeated and victorious—I want you to cut me, sharpen me. I want to drink tea beside you in ten years or a thousand. Flowers grow far away on a planet they'll call Cephalus, and these flowers bloom once a century, when the living star and its black-hole binary enter conjunction. I want to fix you a bouquet of them, gathered across eight hundred thousand years, so you can draw our whole engagement in a single breath, all the ages we've shaped together.

I veer rhapsodic; my prose purples. And yet I don't think you'll laugh, or if you do, the laughter would delight me. Maybe I've over-read the simple word with which you close your letter. (But I can never over-read you, and the word you chose is not simple.) Maybe I overstep your bounds. And, to be honest, love confuses me. I've never felt it before this—I've had joy in sex; I've had fast friendships. Neither feels right for this, and this feels bigger than both. So let me say what I mean, as well as I can.

I sought loneliness when I was young. You've seen me there: on my promontory, patient and unaware.

But when I think of you, I want to be alone together. I want to strive against and for. I want to live in contact. I want to be a context for you, and you for me.

I love you, and I love you, and I want to find out what that means together.

Love,

Red

———————————————————————

Commandant summons Red to a field office.

Blood, as usual, is everywhere. Mostly frozen, this time, which smells better.

The Agency has chosen a Russian front close to the main braid, where the Nazis have some trick of raising the dead—nothing supernatural, but nature has strange forms C20 scientists rarely guess. The gnawing corpses have a sharp, fungal odor when Red draws close enough, which suggests down-thread intervention, the great adversary at work. The sky is mostly white, but the snow has stopped for now, and clear blue opens high up and far away.

The Soviet soldiers are scared and cold and hungry. They will die here. They will hold their post just long enough for Zhukov to reinforce another, more critical position behind them. They are brave boys and more than a few girls. They share their last spirits—songs, jokes from home, whatever they carry in their flasks. Bravery won't save them. Neither will the gallows-grim gravity their officers' faces wear.

Other operatives appear and disappear, carrying reports or cases of weaponry or their comrades' blanched, drained bodies. They bear trophies and tribute. Everyone looks scared. They fit right in.

Altogether, a well-chosen office.

Usually Commandant operates upthread from some gleaming crystal citadel or other. At times the Agency has called Red to report to a bare platform orbiting an unfamiliar star, forgetting even to produce a humanlike superior she can address. The stars alone listen.

Commandant must have been decanted once—all her agents had. But she retreated to her pod long ago and now roams time and space as a disembodied mind, wedded to, webbed through, the Agency's great hyperspace machines. She takes form only when she must, and when she does, she chooses any form that lies to hand, or none. Mostly she contemplates abstracts and calculates trajectories in time, considers her many agents as multidimensional vectors and knots. Viewed from sufficient height, all problems are simple. All knots can be untied with a few deaths, or ten thousand.

Such remove has its place when the fight goes well. Decisions made far from the front are secure against insurgence, infiltration.

Passing corpses, Red wraps herself more tightly in her coat. Not to guard her flesh—she is barely cold, even in this death freeze—but to guard the small blue flame inside her.

Loss begs immediate response. Decisions lose the luxury of distance. Commandant remains downthread, of course, but she's made a local copy for moment-to-moment operations, damage containment, scouting, and that copy has climbed the braid into the past to chart the new threads Garden's spun, the strands it has shifted, the knots it has tied.

Field offices are vulnerable, however. So they are built in bubbles of time, fortified against causes and effects.

Red walks past three men struggling to restrain their fallen, infected comrade, past the doctor trying to stitch a cold-numbed wound with freezing fingers, and she knows that whatever happens here, all this will pass, and all these people die.

Fitting.

Red ducks through the flap of the command tent.

Commandant stands before her, in the form of a big woman in an army uniform, wearing an apron, with bloody pliers in one hand. She holds them as if she is not used to holding things. Adjutants cluster near, bearing their reports on clumsy period tech: paper, mimeograph, map. A man sits unconscious, tied to a wooden chair, naked, bleeding from the mouth. The tent is warmer than outside, but it is not warm enough. His half-open eyes are lapis deep.

Red salutes.

"Get out," Commandant tells her staff, and out they go. The man remains. He does not make a sound. Perhaps he does not notice, or he hopes they will not notice him.

For all practical purposes, they are alone. Red waits. Commandant paces. Her hands are bloody, and she does not seem to notice or care. Stolen worry lines her face. Those lines belong to the woman whose body Commandant now rides, but they suit her. The war has turned hard. Red imagines how those pliers would feel in her own mouth, closing around her own molars or canines, and decides: *If that's how this goes, fine.* She keeps the flame inside her safe.

"We're in bad shape," Commandant says. "Long, careful work on the adversary's part, traps upthread and down, all executed by a single operative, triggering a cascade. I'd call it brilliant if it hadn't put us so far on the back foot. But we count our blessings: Their new braid is weak. We can unpick it. And we will." Commandant glances over, seems surprised. "At ease. Didn't I say, at ease?"

Red stands at ease. Commandant's uncertainty on so small a point as this worries her. Should she be worried? Isn't she a traitor now?

"We've plotted a solution, through math and cruder methods." She sets the pliers on a table, takes up a piece of paper, and offers it to Red. "Do you recognize this woman?"

It is not easy to remain at ease. She takes the paper and makes herself look at the charcoal drawing the way someone would if searching their memory for a face glimpsed across a battlefield, then forgotten. It occurs to Red, as she ponders the face that dwells within her dreams, that this is longer than she has ever dared to watch this particular face, in person— or even to linger on her memory.

The man in the chair whimpers.

Red doesn't blame him. What does Commandant know? Is this a trap? If they knew, wouldn't they kill her? Or do their plans run deeper?

"I recognize her," she says, at last. "From the field. I saw this face in the battle at Abrogast-882. She has others." But always there's a similar stillness about the eyes and a cruel, clever twist to the mouth. She shines through. Red does not say that last part.

"That's where our observers took this likeness."

The tent, suddenly, feels colder than outside. Observers. How long? What have they seen? She remembers her battle with the shadow. "I take it this is the operative who triggered the cascade."

"And set it. Effective, and dangerous. As dangerous as you, in her own way."

An opening. "I'll raise her to the top of my target list." And we will hunt and hunt in turn.

"Turn over the drawing," Commandant says.

When Red took the paper, its back side was blank. Now it holds a multicolored snarl she is far more used to visualizing in three dimensions. She blurs her eyes, crosses them slightly, and topology emerges from the multicolor mess. A green thread, which she thinks should be blue, runs down the core of the braid—but it swerves here and there to intersect another, which is gray and should be red. How much ignorance can she fake and remain convincing? "I don't understand."

"So far as we can trace it, her paths upthread and down have formed this new braid's core. But in these deviations, well—this gray line represents your own course."

"We faced each other at Abrogast-882," Red says. "Also, I think, in Samarkand." What else would Commandant know? She sees through abstraction, tension, weight, through propositions and counterarguments. "Beijing." How can Red explain away this topology that brings her, time and again, near Blue? She thinks and tries to look like she is not thinking.

"You mistake me," Commandant replies. "We believe your paths have crossed because she has gone out of her way to cross them. Often subtly: upthread or down, alterations so small as to be almost undetectable."

"What are you saying?" She knows what Commandant is saying, but she also knows what part she has to play.

"This operative has been grooming you. Her behavior suggests a fondness for grand gesture. You are being played.

Subtly, perhaps so subtly you do not realize it yourself. Her masters want a weakness in our ranks."

It could be true. It's not, but it could be. She knows it's not. She does. "I'm loyal." This is not, as a rule, something loyal people say, but Commandant is too lost in thought to notice.

"We believe she wants to turn you. She's seeding dissatisfaction. Little sense details you might not even notice. She is not trying to kill you: We have scanned you and found you clean."

When was the scan? Who delivered it? What else did they find?

"She is waiting for you to make an overture: to ask her a question, to initiate contact. Something so subtle it could plausibly escape our observations. That message is our gate. Through that, we strike."

Outside, a lone artillery piece fires for some reason. Red's ears ring. The man in the chair moans. Commandant does not flinch. She does not know she's supposed to. Red should not feign stupidity before this woman, but she needs the time an explanation will buy her. "What do you suggest?"

"Are you familiar," Commandant asks, "with genetic steganography?"

This is one of those questions Red is not expected to answer.

"Our finest minds will help you craft the message. We will end her, and end the threat—without its linchpin, our adversary's recent work will be easily unpicked. You are critical to the war effort, agent." Commandant takes a sealed letter from the desk and offers it to her. She holds the letter too tight, since she's unused to having hands. Red accepts. Bloodstains linger on the envelope, and the paper's dimpled and creased with the strength of Commandant's grip. "Suspend your ongoing operations. Transfer to the thread indicated here. Begin the work. Save the world."

"Yes, sir." Red salutes again.

Commandant returns the salute, then hefts the pliers again. The man on the chair is already screaming by the time Red leaves.

A comrade raises his hand, wants to talk to her. Red marches out to her duty. She makes it ten threads over, a continent away, several centuries up, before she collapses at the foot of an enormous rainbowed wall of water called Mosi-oa-Tunya and does not weep.

She watches with her eyes open.

Some time later, a bee zips past her ear and dances before her, amid the spray. She reads the letter it writes on air and feels a sickness around the flame in her chest. They can make this work. They have to.

At the end, she holds out her hand. The bee settles on it and jabs its stinger into her palm.

Later, when Red is gone, a small, uncommonly adventurous spider seizes the corpse. Then, when the spider's eaten its fill, Seeker eats the spider.

My Heart's Own Blood,

I dance to you in a body built for sweetness, a body that tears itself apart in defense of what it loves. This letter will sting you when it's done. Let it, and read a postscript in its death throes.

I dance—this will be a very boring letter—because this thing in me, this piping heat, this rising sun that hardly fits in the sky of me won't stay put. To know you my equal in this, too—this beat of my blood's drum, this feast that won't diminish no matter how I ravage it—Red. Red, Red, Red, I want to write you poetry, and I am laughing, understand, as I teach this small body my joy, laughing at the joke of me and the relief, the relief of being supine on a stone slab with a knife above me and seeing your hand and eyes guiding it.

That surrender should be satiety. That it should have taken me this long to learn that.

Red, I love you. Red, I will send you letters from everywhen telling you so, letters of only one word, letters that will brush your cheek and grip your hair, letters that will bite you, letters that will mark you. I'll write you by bullet ant and spider wasp; I'll write you by shark's tooth and scallop shell; I'll write you by virus and the salt of a ninth wave flooding your lungs; I'll—

stop, here, I'll stop. This is probably not how this is done. I want flowers from Cephalus and diamonds from Neptune, and I want to scorch the thousand earths between us to see what blooms from the ash, so we can discover it hand in hand, content in context, intelligible only to each other. I want to meet you in every place I have loved.

I don't know how it's done between such as us, Red. But I can't wait to find out together.

Love,

Blue

PS. I write to you in stings, Red, but this is me, the truth of me, as I do so: broken open by the act, in the palm of your hand, dying.

If Blue were less of a professional, she might sing as she slices the throat of her mark, tucked comfortably beneath Hôtel La Licorne's brocade bedclothes and silk sheets she is almost sorry to spoil. The easiest work since her great achievement, and all in her favourite strands; Blue almost feels herself on vacation, she is so relaxed, so happy. Others work, now, to tend the new shoot, while she cuts fresh swathes in soft flesh.

She does not sing—but the bright bubbling of the earl's blood beneath her hands makes her sigh, and ballads crowd her tongue. *O, the earl was fair to see!*

Blue has never laid plans, not really. Not her own, ever. Her job is to execute (she almost laughs, washing her hands, but doesn't), to perform. She is familiar with cautionary poets' exhortations across half a dozen strands, of mice, men, plans, canals, Panama—but she plans, now. She sits at the octagonal mirror in her own room—which she never left by the door, naturally, honestly the penny dreadful of her actions is another layer of amused enjoyment for her—and braids her dark hair in slow, careful configuration. She lays a circuitry of colour over the strands, raises a map out of them, and thinks of surfaces, of opposites that match, of the breathtaking reciprocity of a reflection. She curates, idly, scenarios in which to receive and deliver conversation, as one hand crosses another.

She has won, which is not an unfamiliar feeling. She is happy, which is.

She takes the stairs to meet her alibi for a drink, smiling, already thinking ahead to the cognac she glimpsed earlier in the day, the reddest one, and how it will fill her mouth with sweet fire.

Garden looks out at her from the alibi's eyes.

Blue does not miss a beat, but the smooth legato into which she folds the beat may as well be a stumble to Garden. Blue's fingers curl around the gilt back of a chair as slowly as the corners of her lips curl into a smile. She pulls it out, sits down, while Garden pours her a glass of red wine to match her own.

"I hope you don't mind my dropping in," says Garden, mischievous green gaze flicking up at Blue, "but I so wanted to toast to our success in person. As it were."

Blue chuckles and reaches her hand across the table to

clasp Garden's, warmly. "It's good to see you. As it were."
Blue withdraws her hand, reaches for her glass, raises an eyebrow. "But you're concerned about something."

"The toast, first." Garden raises her glass; Blue mirrors
her. "To lasting success." Their glasses clink; they sip. Blue
closes her eyes as she licks colour from her lips, obliterates its
name even as she coats her tongue with it, listens to the deep
velvety green of Garden's voice.

"You're in danger," says Garden, in soft, almost apologetic
tones. "I want to put you to bed."

Blue opens her eyes and affects a look of mild surprise.
"That's very flattering, but I expect a lady to buy me dinner first."

Garden's laugh is a rustle of leaves. She leans forward,
and Blue feels herself falling into her eyes, tasting the ease
they promise, the rest.

"My dear," says Garden, "your accomplishment, while
stellar, has a touch of, shall we say, ostentation to it. Relatively
speaking. Where your siblings bloom and melt back into me,
you . . ." Garden brushes a soft thumb along Blue's cheek with
a tenderness that draws a tremble from her jawline. "You root
in the air, my epiphyte. It's no hard thing to trace the new
growth to you, singly. You have always," says Garden, planting
the words into Blue's smile like strangler fig, "been too fond
of signing your work."

If Blue were less of a professional, she might have looked

stunned. She might have chewed her lip. She might have walled up the inside of herself into a tomb and drowned it in a bog and set the bog on fire in her panic of what and when and how long.

Instead, she rakes through Garden's words, look, tone, tills their depths, and turns over nothing but affectionate reproof of longstanding habit. She leans forward, takes Garden's hands in hers again.

"If you embed me now," she says, steadily, "we commit to losing the ground we've gained. More slowly, yes, but it will be a step sideways instead of forward. Keep me in, and we can press this advantage. You must feel it—the difference? We're on the brink of something."

"Brinks," says Garden, with casual fondness, "are traditionally stepped back from."

"They are also fine places over which to tip one's enemies," says Blue. "Traditionally."

Garden chuckles, and Blue knows she's won. "Very well. Once you're done here, proceed upthread until you meet my sign, then twelve strands over. There's a delicate opportunity there." Garden draws her hands back slowly. "You are more precious than you know, my tumbleweed. Take care."

Then Garden is gone, and Blue makes a dry remark about the strength of the wine as her alibi finds her focus again, laughs, and the evening dissolves into mirth.

When Blue checks out the next morning, the concierge looks confused. "My apologies, mademoiselle," he says. "There has been a mistake with your bill—I will make up another—"

"May I," says Blue, not trembling, not in knots, gloved hand sure as she reaches for it, already seeing the smudge in the ink for what it is, disguised as an unlikely decimal point. She reads it while the concierge looks on.

"Ah, yes," she says, her voice warm and bright. "My friend and I enjoyed ourselves a little too well last night, but so fine a champagne would have been a step too far. You are correct." She smiles. "We had nothing to celebrate."

She crumples the smudged bill neatly before the concierge can ask for it back, pays the new bill, walks out, and imagines the housekeeper's scream in one hour's time in place of her own. A groundskeeper burns brush outside; Blue tosses the old bill into the blaze without breaking her stride.

Once she's gone, Seeker plucks the smoldering bill from the flames and eats it piping hot.

Dear Blue—

I can't

   I

   Fuck

   In haste:

   They know.

   Not everything. Not yet.

But they know you. Your hammer blow, your trap, your triumph, your emergence—you hurt them bad, and they won't let you have another shot. Not ever.

They know you're close to me. Somehow they mapped us, our earliest beginnings, in spite of all our care. They don't have the letters—I don't think—just your interest, our nearness in time. They feel it through the strands, like spiders. They think you want to turn me. Did you, once? Was that why you reached for me at the first, whatever we've become since?

They think you're waiting for me to contact you. To send you a letter. I can't even laugh. They have machines to rewrite the code of cells, to turn proteins the wrong way round. They've never met you, they've never read you, but they know you well enough to break you—if you let them in. And they think if I send you a letter, you'll

I can't write it out. I can't fucking

They're so smart, and so dumb.

Your letter, the sting, the beauty of it. Those forevers you promise. Neptune. I want to meet you in every place I ever loved.

Listen to me—I am your echo.

I would rather break the world than lose you.

I see one solution. It's—it should be—easy.

Let me go. And I'll let you.

I will write their letter. Send it. Do not, under any circumstances, read what you next receive from me. When you do not die, they will see the gambit's lost. Perhaps your interest in me was a feint. Perhaps I wasn't yet ripe for you. Perhaps you spotted the trap before it sprang. Perhaps Commandant was wrong. She has been wrong before, and so have the machines.

Just—don't read what I send you after this. Don't answer.

And we go our separate ways.

I hate it. I never hated before, like I hate this. With all you are to me, and all you'll always be, we can't just go. We can't just walk away.

But I will, if it leaves you living.

They will watch you, and me, closer than ever now. We can fight. We can chase each other down through time, like we did for centuries past before I knew your name. But no more letters. No more of this.

That I should die—fine. I signed on to this war to die.

I don't know if I ever told you that before.

But that you should die. That you should suffer. That they should unmake you.

I love you. I love you. I love you. I'll write it in waves. In skies. In my heart. You'll never see, but you will know. I'll be all the poets, I'll kill them all and take each one's place in turn, and every time love's written in all the strands it will be to you.

But never again like this.

I am so sorry. If I had been stronger. Faster. Smarter. Better. If I had been worth you. If—

You would not want me to curse myself this way.

You'll have to burn this. I hope you can keep

it. I keep the memory. I imagine your hands on the paper. I imagine your fire.

I wish I could hold you.

I love you.

R

Red concocts an ending.

The work takes longer than she thought. She never labored so upon a letter. Day by day she sleeps in the white room and wakes to whiteness and showers alone. Then the experts arrive to help her brew the poison.

The experts rarely speak, and never with her. They wear decontamination suits with faceplates in the lab, while Red goes barefoot. They arrive in the morning and leave at night. Red stays. She peers behind the faceplates while the experts work, and whenever she can see them, they are beautiful and composed, like a house where no one lives, but which a staff cleans daily. She does not think they always looked so calm. Commandant has hollowed them, hallowed them, for this purpose.

Red's message must be subject to minimal interference and oversight, lest the poison reek of committee and warn their prey. That's what Commandant has said. Red does not know whether she should believe.

She proceeds with care.

She never weeps. She does not curse the empty walls of her empty lab, even after the experts have gone home. She does not want to risk Commandant listening.

She sleeps and dreams of letters.

It will be a plant. She chose that form: a plant grown from seed, to give Blue every chance to turn away. She gives it thorns. She makes its berries evil red, its leaves dark and oily. Its every piece cries poison.

She waits for the experts to object, but they do not.

Nothing could be simpler than killing a Garden agent. They die like anyone else—and then their spores infect, their windblown dandelion tufts take seed, their deep roots put forth new shoots. To break them, that's the trick: a brew to snap the chains of memory, tangle the germ line. It must be targeted with care. They have samples of Blue, bits of blood on slides, a strand of hair that might be hers. Before Red can devise a way to steal them, the experts drop them in the pot.

This is a letter of death. It will lack meaning to any but the intended recipient. Its killing words will lace through Red's message, hidden, until the charm's wound up. Steganography: hidden writing. Writing inside other writing.

She writes, on the first level, a simple enough note, the

note Commandant expects her to write: an expression of interest; a temptation and a dare. Not unlike the letter Blue wrote her back then.

She thinks, *Do not read this.*

She remembers how it felt so long ago to taunt her, to rejoice in victory. Blueberry. Blue-da-ba-dee. Mood Indigo. She tries to channel that memory against all that's happened since.

She can't.

She thinks, *Some time traveler I am.*

Blue won't fall for this. She will listen. She received the letter. She will understand. She must. The only future they have is one apart and together. They lived for so long without knowing one another, warring through time. They were separate, they did not speak, but each shaped the other, even as they were shaped in turn.

So just go back to that. Why not?

It will hurt. They've hurt before, to save each other's lives.

But there is another path. One she cannot bear to chart, and yet she must, because while Blue is subtle, she is also bold, and this may be the last chance Red will have.

So when the experts have left, she hides another message in the message they have hidden inside hers. She frames new meaning in the poison lines and hides it so the techs won't notice, so even Commandant won't see. She hopes.

Steganography is hidden writing. You hide a message in a crossword puzzle, a novel, a work of art, in the dapple of a dawn river. Even your hidden message can hide other messages deeper, as here. Eat one of the berries Red has made, and you would find a simple message, and inside that message, the poison. And inside the poison, farther down, legible only as in death, she hides another letter. A true letter.

To think of this letter being read sickens her, but she writes it anyway, because whatever happens next, this is the end.

Because it is the end, she cannot resist the urge to make this deadly thing beautiful.

The seed has its luster. Growing, she lends it fragrance. Blossoming, she grants it color, depth. Berrying, she gives it shine and taste. Even its thorns are wicked art. She signs her death with love.

She must, even now, give Blue something worthy of her.

Blue will not read it. She will spot the trap.

All will be well.

And they will go back to how they were before.

Nothing need change, though everything has.

They can make this work.

When it is done, she sleeps, restless.

The next day they close the lab. It's due to be destroyed: a bomb, a footnote of history. Red watches the explosion. She was ordered to save no one. She saved a few anyway, what deaths history could spare.

In the blooming dust she reads a letter.

She walks away.

Later, a shadow moves among the ashes, eating.

Dear Red,

As you wish.

B

Blue stands among the groundlings, watching players strut and fret their hour upon the stage.

She's an apothecary's apprentice in this life, a study in dark and bright: black hair cropped short beneath a flat felt cap, black doublet over white shirt and hose. She has carried out Garden's delicate opportunity—one womb quickened, another slowed—and lingers, now, on the margins, watching the first performance of a new play.

If Blue were a scholar—and she has played one enough times to know she would have loved to be—she would catalogue, across all strands, a comprehensive study of the worlds in which *Romeo and Juliet* is a tragedy, and in which a comedy. It delights her, whenever visiting a new strand, to take in a performance not knowing how it will end.

She is not delighted now. She watches the performance with all the tense fervor of awaiting prophecy.

She leaves before the end.

She returns to the shop. A plant—a curious cross, her master said, between hemlock and yew—sits potted near a window. Dark, oily leaves; viciously elegant thorns; berries red as the half-moons she digs into her palms every time she looks at them.

The letter is beautifully composed. She is not.

This, more than anything, infuriates her.

She has grown it, dutifully, from a seed—oddly marked, misshapen, glinting blue in a paper packet of pale browns. She has watched for a year—while she coaxed life into one belly and banished it from another—its mocking growth into a promise never kept, a sheet of music never played.

The plant is written in an obvious geomantic script, a kind of crude binary culled from Levantine manuscripts. The number of needles and berries on a branch form divinatory figures—*conjunctio, puella*—whose names can be easily parsed for a more elaborate alphabet. *Dear Blue, I've thought about your proposal but need a demonstration of trust. It's risky for me to communicate with you, so I've disguised the real letter as poison—consume it, and you'll know when to meet me and where.*

It doesn't even sound like her. The thought of some grey-faced Agency hack hovering over Red's shoulder as she writes fills her mouth with helpless fury. In dreams, sometimes, Blue sees herself straddling the goon, punching their face into pulp, except her hands keep slipping off, sliding away, and she can't land a hit, and the goon laughs and laughs until a plant grows out of their mouth and says Blue's name.

On her good days, she pricks her fingers experimentally on the thorns and thinks of spindles. On her bad days she takes trips seventy years downthread just to watch London burn.

Today is a very bad day.

A berry dropped. She nearly screamed—suppose it were a paragraph?—and picked it from the soil, held it between thumb and forefinger, placed it in her palm, made certain it hadn't been pierced on a thorn, lost an ant's sip of juice. It wasn't yet time, she thought; a year is nothing, a year is no time at all to wait for a letter rescinding the letter, a letter contradicting the contradiction of this letter. The deadline for reply is written in the plant's own mortality.

Truth be told, Blue is insulted. How obvious; how unsubtle. Red said not to read her next letter—and here it is, announcing itself as poison as a test of Blue's interest, of Red's success. If Blue eats it, she'll die—but if Blue doesn't, then Red's side will know she's been tipped off, will suspect Red, will destroy her instead.

Her heart should have been broken by better. Her

betrayal should have had sharper teeth. All that—all that. And now this.

Still, she strokes its leaves. Still, she bends to sniff the stems: a blend of cinnamon and rot.

She was always going to eat it down to the root.

There are as many berries as they have exchanged letters. She eats each one slowly, her eyes closed, crushing some against her hard palate, others between her teeth, rolling their sweetness along her tongue. They have bitter, varied aftertastes, and the numbing properties of clove—frustrating when the thorns begin to tear into her cheeks and throat. She wants to feel everything.

She thinks of ortolan as she chews the plant's fibres, considers draping her head in white cloth for closer communion. She wipes bright blood from her lips and laughs, softer and softer, swallowing every stroke of flavour.

She thinks, *Loathsome in its own deliciousness.*

She wipes tears from her face and feels them mix stickily with her blood. She thinks she feels, stirring in her, a counter-clockwise twist against her being.

She rises, washes her face, washes her hands, and sits down to write a letter.

Stop.

Blue. I mean it.

I love you. But stop. Don't read this. Each word is murder.

Dearest Blue, beloved Blue, wise fierce foolish Blue, don't shrug this danger off as you've shrugged off death and time before. This is no slight sidling risk, no road-met random monster, no dragon, no woodland beast, no alien god to trick or out-war. Nothing so kind. These are words made to unmake you, and well wrought. You'll have no second coming after this.

Put the letter down. We'll have each other still, as memories and rivals. We'll confront ourselves in the chase through time as it was when I first learned the shape of you. We can still dance, as enemies. Just stop now, and live and love and let be.

Stop, my love. Stop. Find a purgative, a hospital, a shaman-priest, one of your healing cocoons—there's time. Barely.

Goddamn it, stop.

Each line I write, I must imagine you reading—
and imagine what has made you read so far, ignoring
my advice, as your body revolts and poison claims
you. It twists in my guts. If you have read this far, I
am not worth you. I am a coward. I let them use me.
If you have read this far, I have been made a weapon,
and they have plunged me into your heart.

I am so weak.

Give me up. Leave now. There's still a chance—
however slim. I love you. I love you. I love you.

Go.

Forever yours,

Red

And yet you're still here. Aren't you. Immune to
my ruses, Indigo. I hoped you would leave and
save yourself. But you remain. I think I would too.
I hope I would be that brave, if you are. That we
each would give up as much to read the other's last
few lines, written in water and forever.

I love you. If you've come this far, that's all I
can say. I love you and I love you and I love you,
on battlefields, in shadows, in fading ink, on cold ice

splashed with the blood of seals. In the rings of trees. In the wreckage of a planet crumbling to space. In bubbling water. In bee stings and dragonfly wings, in stars. In the depths of lonely woods where I wandered in my youth, staring up—and even then you watched me. You slid back through my life, and I have known you since before I knew you.

I know your solitude and poise, the clenched fist of you, the blade: a glass shard in Garden's green glowing world. And yet you'd never fit in mine. I wish I could have shown you where I'm from, hand in hand, the world I set out to build and to protect—I don't think you would have liked it, but I want to see it reflected in your eyes. I wish I could have seen your braid, and I wish we could have left all those horror shows behind and found one together, for ourselves. That's all I want now. A small place, a dog, green grass. To touch your hand. To run my fingers through your hair.

I don't even know how that feels, and you're—

I'm sorry. No. If we're this far, if you've been this selfish—I did not mean that. I would have fought you forever. I would have wrestled you through time. I would have turned you, and been turned. I would do anything. I have done so much, and would have done as much again, and more. And yet here I am, a fool, writing you one last time, and here you are, a fool, reading me. We're one, at least, in folly.

I hope you never read these words. I sicken to write them; I know how it will hurt you to reach this far. It is always too late to say what must be said. I cannot stop you now. I cannot save you. Love is what we have, against time and death, against all the powers ranged to crush us down. You gave me so much—a history, a future, a calm that lets me write these words though I'm breaking. I hope I've given you something in return—I think you would want me to know I have. And what we've done will stand, no matter how they weave the world against us. It's done now, and forever.

What will I do, sky? Lake, what? Bluebird, iris, ultramarine, how can there be more when this is done? But it will never end—that's the answer. There is always us.

Dearest, deepest Blue— At the end as at the start, and through all the in-betweens, I love you.

Red

Red arrives too late.

She should not come at all. Commandant will watch closely, for this is her triumph, long awaited. Red does not care.

She so rarely dreams, but did tonight, of players and an empty stage, of Blue crushing a poison berry between her teeth, and on waking, Red screamed, sweaty, death-mouthed, wide awake uncertain, as if a pane of glass within her soul had cracked. Terror seized her. She will not trust history or the report of spies.

Threads burn as you enter them. She cuts herself out of the air onto a shit-stinking muddy street in some upthread Albion, unwarmed by weak sun in a sky the color of whey. She wears trousers, a long coat, sheer gloves; to locals' eyes she might as well be naked. Her passage makes waves. She will not be here long. Garden, panicked, slithers shoots upthread to catch her, chase her, kill her; Commandant, feeling this, sends her own agents in pursuit.

Fuck them.

She knows the shop, has observed it from afar, and barges through into a haze, cloying smells of drying fruit and herbs and heavy metals, every wall hung with bushes in some state of desiccation. The master alchemist consults a tear-streaked–widow client; they stare at Red in shock, in fear, and she locks them in place with a gesture of her gloves. Climbs the stairs, finds the prentice's room. Knocks once, growls, slaps the door off its hinges.

And there she lies, sprawled upon the bed.

She might be asleep, wrapped in sunlight, but she is not. Blood has congealed already. Red wanted the poison to be painless, but Garden's people—Blue's—hold to life, and breaking that hold takes savagery. Blue fought to— Red can't bear to think the word "die" at first, but that's hypocrisy. This is her fault. The least she can do is own it. Start again:

Blue fought to die composed. Red only sees the pain because she knows to look for it and knows, too, how Blue looks when she's hiding something.

The face, still. The jaw clenched, lips softly parted. The chest does not rise or fall. The eyelids parted, whites visible and shot through with blood.

One hand clasps a letter to her breast. On the letter,

Red's name. Her real name. Blue should not know it. But then, Blue never claimed not to know. A final confession. A final taunt.

The letter is sealed.

The sky should crack.

The world is hollow, its many braids chewing-gum snarls of nonsense. Let them die.

Red falls to her knees by the bed. She runs her hand through Blue's hair and grips it between her fingers, and it does not feel the way she imagined, and that is the last sick joke. She clutches it and feels the skull, and the stillness, and lets her own sobs choke her into silence.

The sky changes color outside the window. Vines sprout from dead floorboards. Alarms are ringing in the ordered Garden and through the Agency's cold halls. Agents exposed, endangered, dead. Monsters climb upthread to find her, kill her, save her.

She clutches Blue and feels her cold and stiff. The world trembles, and the sky darkens. Garden may burn this whole strand, rather than let its infection descend.

But by some coward's instinct, as the sky goes black and the screams begin outside, Red grabs the letter and runs.

She is fast and fierce, and unlike her pursuers she does not care if she never finds her way home again. She slips from thread to thread. Cities bloom and decay around her. Stars die. Continents shift. Everything starts, and everything fails.

She finds herself on a cliff at the world's end. Mushroom clouds flower on the horizon as some remnant of a remnant of man wipes itself out.

Her hands shake as they raise the letter. The seal is a blot, a dot, an ending. It laughs at her, red as Red as red and hungry, and she wants teeth to crouch beneath, a cave that is a mouth where she can hide and be eaten and swallowed and gone. This is the last of it. Blue should have listened. She should have run. How could she die like this? How could she die at all?

The tears have anger in them at first, but anger burns out fast. Tears stay.

She slides her finger beneath the flap and pulls. The seal breaks as easy as a spine.

She reads.

Around her the world burns. Plants wither. The waves wash carcasses ashore.

Red screams at the sky. She calls Beings in which she does not believe to account. She wants there to be a God, so she can curse Her.

She reads again.

Radiation wind blows through her. Hidden organs wake to keep her alive.

A shadow stands behind her.

Red turns and looks.

She has never seen the seeker before, her shadow; even now she sees only outline, distortion, crystal slipped into a clear river—and a hand, outstretched. No Agency creature after all—and no Garden thing, either. This should be a mystery, an unveiling of secrets—an answer.

What does it matter? she thinks. *What does any of it matter?*

She presses the letter into that glassy, reaching hand and steps off the cliff.

She holds to her despair as rocks streak past and other rocks approach and the sky's a ruin of bombs, but at the last breath before impact she breaks. This is too good for her, too easy, too quick. Blue wouldn't grace her with a death this clean. And she's always been a coward.

Weeping, cursing, broken, a hair's breadth from the rocks, she slips away into the past.

Oh, Red.

The twist of you in me. The writhe. You're a whip uncoiling in my veins, and I write between the rearing and the snap.

Of course I write to you. Of course I ate your words.

I will try to compose myself—to order myself into something you can read. I fall to paper and quill because there is no time, now, to do anything else—and it is luxury, in its own way, to do this. To write in plain sight. To write, too, to the rhythm of what I feel happening. It's fascinating, in its own way. It's everything I wanted from an enemy. I wish you could hear me clap.

Brava, my pomegranate. Well done. Nine out of ten.

(I reserve a point, always, to encourage reach exceeding grasp.)

The ache in the back teeth is an interesting touch. I've been through the cold sweats, and now I think my hands are starting to shake, so I pray you'll forgive the flaws in penmanship. You should read your triumph in them.

I was disappointed at first, you know—the obviousness of the double-bluff. Methought you did protest too much. But it worked, after all—I bit your poisoned apple. There'll be no glass coffin for me—all your Shift could ever have been—and certainly no necrophilic prince to tumble me into a different story.

You'd have made such a splendid agent for our side, truly. If anything saddens me in this, it's the waste of you—sweet and safe in cold sharp places that won't thrill to pierce your skin.

The needle sinks and spirals through its grooves. I spurt anachronisms as I wind down. It's good to feel this in common with the universe, somehow. I never died but once—that once I told you of—and it was quite a different thing. Strange how being erased can bring one in line with a greater narrative.

I loved you. That was true. With what's left of me I can't help but love you still. This is how you win, Red: a long game, a subtle hand played well. You played me like a symphony, and I hope you won't mind my feeling a little proud of you for such a magnificent betrayal.

I see you now as the red hourglass on a black widow's back, measuring out my life in cooling blood. I imagine you coming upon whatever will be left of my body, spinning your nanite-shrouds to break, learn, consume my remains. I expect it to be exhaustingly tidy. Boring, even. I certainly hope I'll be dead by then.

The pain truly is excruciating. It's wonderful, really. Is this what it's like to not feel hungry anymore? A lot less work than the other way. Wish I could go back upthread and—

I think this is it. I need to keep strength enough to seal this. What would Mrs. Leavitt say otherwise? Or Bess, or Chatterton?

Thank you, Red. It was a hell of a ride.

Take care my yew berry, my wild cherry, my foxglove.

Yours,

Blue

Red kills time.

She strides through the veils of the past, a woman robed in fire, hands wet with enemy blood. Her fingernail razor blades slide through the meat of your back; she stalks you as a shadow down long lonely halls, footsteps metronome measured, inescapable. She visits dark-angel mercies on the curled metal wrecks of Mombasa and Cleveland.

Commandant chided her for exposing herself back in the apothecary's shop, but Red claimed she had to see, to know for sure the threat was done. Did Commandant believe her? Perhaps not. Perhaps survival is its own form of torture.

She has lost all the subtlety Blue ever teased her for lacking, her old competitive patience for a good officer's work. She abandons her tools, retreats to the grossest physical foundations. Winning this battle, losing that, strangling that old evil man in a bathtub in his skyscraper penthouse, feels empty because it is: In the war they wage through time, what lasting advantage comes from murdering ghosts, who, with a slight shift of threads, will return to life or live different lives that never bring them to the executioner's blade? Repetitive task, murder. Kill them and kill them again, like weeds, all the little monsters.

No death sticks but the one that matters.

She is useless to the war effort like this. Might as well shovel snow. But she is a hero, and heroes can shovel snow if they like.

Garden sends weapons against her, stinking green, howling sideways down strange angles from alien braids into the ghost land she walks, fit partners to kill or die.

She visits Europe, because Blue liked it here.

She thinks that name in her head now. What risk?

She sees London built and burning, upthread and down; she sits atop Saint Paul's and drinks tea and watches madmen drop bombs while other madmen skitter over lead rooftops to put the fires out. She chucks spears in revolts against the Romans. She sets a great fire in a plague year. In another thread, she puts that fire out. She lets a mob tear her. She walks cholera-stricken streets while Blake scribbles apocalypses upstairs. The Tube still runs, in some threads, long after the city falls to robots or riot or is merely abandoned, all that beloved history a cast-off shell for beings who stride godlike skyward, and she rides it, rusting, empty, in circles, smelling a rot she cannot place. Coward, the rails call her—small use fighting now. Coward to continue, and coward to seek an end.

Even an immortal can only ride the Circle line so long. She wanders dripping tunnels, paced by swarms of scuttling sentient rats—they stink and hiss, their tails slither over brick, and she wishes they would fight her. They are not so foolish, or else they're cruel. She collapses to her knees, and the rat tide closes over her, whiskers sharp against her cheeks; tails curl around her ears, and when the tide passes she is crying again, and though she never had a mother, she thinks she knows what a mother's touch would feel like.

She remembers sun. She remembers sky.

Red cannot stay below forever. She does not know why she chooses the station she does, but she leaves the tracks and climbs.

She will see the city one last time, and then.

Even composed, certain, she cannot frame the *then*.

She stops, her hand on the bannister, overcome by—not those old French stairway spirits, but the other ones that whisper in your ear as you climb to a familiar room, that if you knock, if the door is opened, your world will change.

After a long time, she realizes she has been staring at a mural. A copy of an old painting, made to advertise a museum long since burned to ash. It survives here, in a subway like a bunker.

A boy dies on a bed, by a window.

One hand claws his still breast, the other trails on the floor. He is beautiful, and he wears blue trousers.

Red staggers back against the wall.

The window half-open. The slumped coat beside the bed. The open box. Hips turned half up. Every detail of pose is right, save only the absence of letter and the fact that the boy upon the bed in the mural does not look like Blue at all. For one thing, his hair is red.

Terror seizes Red beneath the earth. She thinks, *This must be a trap.* She feels herself seen by a mind far subtler and vast. But, if it's a trap, why is she still alive? What game is this, sapphire? What slow victory, o heart of ice?

The dead boy remains.

The undoing of latter-century forgers. Chatterton, that Marvellous Boy.

And she realizes: Blue would not kill her. She knows this. She has always known.

So, why? A taunt? I will write myself into the world, so you will see me throughout all braids and mourn?

And yet. Red did not recognize the reference to this painting—and neither would Commandant. For Commandant, art is a curiosity, a detour on the journey to pure math.

Red thinks of steganography, of hidden letters, of the rings of trees.

I will try to compose myself—to order myself into something you can read.

She remembers that last letter. A *long game*, she wrote, *a subtle hand played well.* Remembers *between the rearing and the snap.* Remembers *pomegranate*, and what pomegranates are for.

They stick in the throat. They scatter to a hundred seeds. They bring daughters of earth back down to the land of death—but death does not claim them.

What is this, but a small mind's deluded fantasy? What is this, but clutching straws against death and time?

What is love, ever, but—

Wish I could go back upthread, Blue wrote.

Red thinks, *There is a chance.*

A chance? Call it a trap, a temptation, suicide with a kind face. Any of those would be nearer the truth.

All that supposing Blue even sent this message—that Red has not manufactured it, groping in despair for meaning in broken images the next braid's twist will wash away. Art comes and goes in the war. The painting on the subway wall might be an accident. She might be making this up.

But.

There is a chance.

Red's poison was built to kill an agent of Garden—like Blue. It would have no purchase on someone of Red's own faction. Someone with her codes, her antibodies, her resistance.

Garden shelters its agents while they grow in embedded crèches ringed with traps. Blue almost died in her childhood crèche—cut off, warped. There is a hole in her mind as a result. And every hole is an opening.

Red has no hope of nearing that crèche as she is. Garden admits only its own.

Blue, as herself, cannot survive. Red, as herself, cannot reach her.

But they have sprinkled bits of themselves through time. Ink and ingenuity, flakes of skin on paper, bits of pollen, blood, oil, down, a goose's heart.

Rocks laid for later avalanches. If you want to change a plant, start from its root.

The plan she's forming offers more ways to die than she can count, and to suffer on the way. If Commandant finds her, she'll hurt long and slow and die babbling hallucinations. If Garden does, she'll be shelled, filleted, and flayed, her mind curled against itself, her fingers snapped and braided. The other side has no more compassion than Red's. She'll have to follow a trail she and Blue rubbed out even as they left it, dodge her foes and former fellows, and then, at the last, walk into the enemy's embrace. In her peak form, there would be no certainty of success.

The decision forms like a jewel in her stomach.

Hope may be a dream. But she will fight to make it real.

She reaches up to touch the dead man's hand upon the wall.

Then she climbs and goes seeking.

Red's no fool: She starts the whole desperate play with autosurgery. She pierces herself with a thin blade bought in thirteenth-century Toledo, breaks the obvious tracking systems. Commandant may yet trace her as she climbs and descends history's braid, but that takes time, and Red moves fast.

The first letter's easy.

They didn't know they were being watched yet, of course. Only rough precautions taken. She emerges from the shadow of a broken gunship and stares into the sky of a world they wrecked and left. The letter is ash; she slits her finger, works blood into the ash to form dough as the world breaks. She applies jeweled lights and odd sounds. She wrinkles time.

Thunder nears. The world cracks through the middle.

The ash becomes a piece of paper, with sapphire writing in a viny hand at the top.

She reads it. She takes the beginning into herself. *This is how we'll win.*

Red finds water in an MRI machine in an abandoned hospital and drinks. In a temple abyss, Red gnaws fallen bones. In a grand computer's heart, she peers through optic circuits. In a frozen waste, she slides a letter's splinters into her skin. She takes them into herself, adapts. Finds all the missing shades of Blue.

As the letters' taunts change tone, she must be more inventive. A spider eating a dragonfly. A shadow drinking tears and coiled enzymes within.

She watches herself weep in a dinosaur swamp, and though she knows this is a trap laid by the younger Red for her shadow follower, the tears still gouge and burn. She cannot stop herself from reaching out, from trying with a touch to say, *I'm here.* Sometimes you have to hold a person, though they'll mistake embrace for strangulation. She wrestles herself in the shadows and feels the pain when she breaks her own hip.

She travels the labyrinth of the past and rereads the letters. Recreates both herself and Blue, so young-seeming now, in her heart.

She clutches the text like a spar against a flood—Red in tooth and claw, the Mongol hordes, curses of Atlantis, a hunger so sharp and bright it might split you open, break a new thing out. Rose-hip tea. Promises of books. *That I might have taught you this.* Tending each to each.

The breadcrumbs she finds as she seeks them! Blodeu-wedd. *You'd need to practically wear their skin.* How long had she planned this? *How long did you know, my mood indigo?*

Or did she know at all? The links are small, deniable. The breadcrumbs could be only crumbs. Red devours them anyway. She has decided; there's no room left for doubt.

Red may be mad, but to die for madness is to die for something.

Commandant's agents smell her, chase her. They trap her in a sinking pirate ship in Coxinga's fleet, and she breaks them quickly, surgically, and peels their camouflage shields away and wears them.

A letter is more than text. She reads Blue into her: tears, breath, skin—most of these traces were scrubbed away, but a few remain. She builds a model of Blue's mind from the words she left; she molds her body to the letters' measure. Almost.

And at last, Red stands on the cliff at the end of the world and holds out her hand, and her heart breaks to see herself weeping in the world before. She wishes she could take herself into her arms, crush her in a fierce embrace.

The broken Red presses Blue's last letter into her hand, jumps off the cliff, and does not die.

The letter remains—the seal, the wax with a drop of blood inside.

On a bare island far upthread, she places the seal upon her tongue, chews, swallows, and collapses.

She shades herself with Blue, from blood, tears, skin, ink, words. She thrashes with the pain of growth inside her: new organs bloom from autosynthesized stem cells to shoulder old bits of her away. Green vines twine her heart and seize it, and she vomits and sweats until the vines' rhythm matches hers. A second skin grows within her skin, popping, blistering. She claws herself off upon the rocks like a snake and lies transformed. And more: A different mind plays around the edges of her own.

She feels herself alien. She has spent thousands of years killing bodies like the one she wears. Sea spray breaks the barren sunrise to rainbows.

Her transformation has not gone unnoticed.

Threads of time sing with the light, swift footfalls of Red's sister-soldiers: The Agency has smelled her treason, their hero turned. She is meat, now, for their teeth.

If they're already that angry, wait until they get a load of her next trick.

She dives from this thread, plummets down the space

between the braids. Time feels different now—she remains herself, but also an echo of her love, a by-blow, a not-quite. The hounds bay behind, Red's sisters, her rivals fiercest and fast, but one by one they realize where she's bound and break off pursuit. The last, too strong and dumb for her own good, remains, nearer, nearer, her hand almost clutching Red's ankle. But the green wall looms ahead, the great border where futures turn from Ours to Theirs.

Red strikes that wall, and it reads the Blue in her, bubbles, at first resists, and she thinks, *That's it, chance failed, we're done.* But then it gapes, and she tumbles through, and it closes fast behind. Her pursuer shatters.

Red falls, flies, down threads she's never dared touch, into Garden.

She enters as a letter, sealed in Blue.

She finds herself, at first, in orbit.

Space here is sick. Thick. Slick. She drowns in cloying honey-heavy light. Her passage through vacuum feels like sliding over meat. The cold touches her new skin but does not burn; her lungs lack air, but she does not need to breathe. Far away and too, too near shines a sun that is an eye with a great hourglass pupil like a goat's, sweeping space for weaknesses to improve, exploit. All the stars are eyes here, always seeking. Red's prophets rail against an indifferent universe; here, in Garden's domain, all the vast worlds care.

The planet she circles has outlived its usefulness, she knows—the new organs tell her. Thick fluid space opens. Green taproots descend from its gaps, wrap the globe, and, with a gentle pruner's strength, crumble it to dirt, drawing life from the fragments until only ash remains. The nutrients are needed elsewhere.

The eye that is a sun sweeps past her, and Red burns with the fury of its glance.

She has made a terrible mistake. She is a fool, and she will die far from home. How could she think she knew this place from letters, from the memories of a friend? How could she have been so certain; how could she believe she'd become enough of Blue to survive here? Not knowing this, did she really know Blue at all?

These are the thoughts that seek to betray her: cracks for roots to exploit.

She thinks of Blue and does not break.

The eye moves on, and so does Red, without betraying her relief.

She walks Garden's many worlds. Space itself is hostile to her here. Moss breathes fumes of sleep; spores drift, seeking traitors' lungs where they can nest. Constellations hang phosphorescent in the sky, and vines tangle between galaxies, great trunk lines bridging stellar gulfs. Life burgeons and blooms even in fusion fires at the heart of stars. She is lost.

She seeks Blue. She climbs through a mangrove growing from a mercury sea, and spiders the size of hands fall on her and tickle the back of her arms, her neck, feather light. They question her in silk, and she answers each challenge with memories of Blue. Blue braiding grasses. Blue taking tea. Blue, hair shorn, come to steal from God. Blue with club raised, Blue with razor, Blue birthing futures.

The spiders mark her with their fangs, which is a dangerous way to give directions. But though the knowledge burns through her veins, the woman Red's become does not die.

She climbs upthread. She works slowly, steps light.

We're grown, I think you know, Blue wrote. *We burrow into the braidedness of time. We are the hedge, entirely, rosebuds with thorns for petals.*

Red finds the place. The spiders' wisdom leads her to a green hollow of vines and moths, where flowers whiter than white bloom, at their hearts only dots of red. She descends into fairyland.

It seems like one of Blue's beloved paintings, but Red can sense the dangers here. The roses waft scents of sleep: *Come rest among us so our thorns can climb through your ears to the softness within.* A blanket of massive gray-wing moths falls from the willow boughs to flutter around her, settle on her, taste her lips with their proboscides. Wings sharper than razors slide rough against her tendons. Grass grows to cushion her steps, but she feels its coiled strength. Is she Blue enough? If this place suspected what she was, she would die at once: carved by mothwing, choked by grass, food for the roses.

But she belongs here. This place belongs to the newness, the Blueness, inside her. So long as she does not fear. So long as she does not waver and gives the grove no reason to suspect.

A mothwing presses, just, between her eyelashes, and she does not scream or vomit or cut her eyeball open.

This is Blue's place. She will not give it the satisfaction of killing her.

Pollen thickens the air with wisdom. To walk is to swim, and so she swims, upthread along the taproot that is this grove, into a past Garden has warded round with walls and thorns to guard the fertile dirt where her most perfect agents grow.

Seeds planted, roots combing through time.

Red swims to the grove's vegetal heart, surrounded by wet, green apparatus through which Garden rears and feeds its tools, its weapons. Yet look another way, with human eyes, and she stands on a hillside near a farm in autumn.

There, the princess lies.

The princess is a creature of thorn and edge and flame. She is a grand weapon unfinished, heartrending and beautiful. Ranks of teeth shine in her mouth.

Look another way, and she is a girl asleep on a hill in light.

When I was very small, Blue wrote, *I got sick*.

When she's grown, she will be fit for a war. But she is not Blue yet.

Red nears. The princess's eyes open, golden, gleaming—and dark, deep, human, both at once, a trap inside a trap. Gorgeous girlmonster, she blinks, stretches between dream and waking.

Red bends to her bed and kisses her.

Her teeth cut Red's lip. Her tongue darts out to claim Red's fallen blood.

Red carved the poison into her memory down those long days in the lab, as she warped berries into paragraphs: a hungry poison, to turn Blue's defenses against her, to make Garden cut her off, to eat her from within.

The blood she gives Blue to drink holds a foretaste of that poison—and Red's antivenom, her resistance. A small virus that, if this works, will taint juvenile Blue the most delicate shade of Red.

I was compromised by enemy action.

Take this of me, Red thinks. *Carry it in yourself, a root fed by what would kill it. Carry hunger all your days. Let it guard you, guide you, save you.*

So that when the world and Garden and I all think you're dead, some part of you will wake. Live. Remember.

If this works.

The gaze of the girl who would be Blue fixes on her, soft with dreams, trusting. She tastes what she is offered, knows the pain in it, and swallows.

Hunger rushes crimson through the girl's veins and out her roots into the glen; it pulses and snaps in flower petals; it sears the wings of moths. The grove burns. Red flees. Burning moths dart for her, carve furrows in her legs and arms and gut, but they cauterize the wounds they carve as they strike. One clips off Red's little finger. Grass catches her leg, ungloves skin from a section of her right calf, but the grass, too, shrivels with hunger, and Red lurches out, bleeding, and gropes upthread toward the home she has betrayed, toward safety that is no longer safe.

But she does not know where else to go.

The slick heavy weight of space is still no longer. Anger tenses the skin of worlds. Eyes that are stars seek a traitor.

Garden chases her.

Red is swift, clever, mighty, and in pain. Free of the grove, subtlety no longer needed, she deploys her armor, her weapons, and makes it a running fight. Suffice to say, this does not go well. The stars that are eyes pin her between possibilities. She wrestles giant taproots in the void. Tearing herself free, she loses armor, bones, fingers, teeth. She calls upon her last secret engines of war, burns the taproots, blinds the eyes— stars collapse and explode at once, and Red falls through a gap in worlds as into a mouth.

She tumbles between threads, in silence and null time, to crash at last, broken, bleeding, barely conscious, in a desert beside two vast and trunkless legs of stone.

She looks up, stares, and, broken-throated, laughs.

And then Commandant's legions fall upon her like the night.

A cell is all Red's world.

They take her from it sometimes to ask her questions. Commandant has so many, all variations on the basic: why, and when, and how, and what. They think they know *who*.

The first time Commandant asked those questions, Red grinned and told her to ask nicely. Then they hurt her.

The second time Commandant asked questions, Red told her, once more, to ask nicely. They hurt her again.

Sometimes they offer pain. Sometimes they offer steak and freedom, a word which means something to them presumably.

But when she's not in use, the world's this cell, this box: gray walls meeting overhead; a flat, gray floor; rounded corners. A bed. A toilet. When she wakes, she finds food on a tray. When they come for her, a door opens at a random point on the curved wall. Her skin is raw. There are hollows beneath it where her weapons used to be.

She suspects they built this prison especially for her. They drag her past other cells, all empty. Perhaps they want her to think she's alone.

The guard comes for her one morning. She has decided to believe whenever she sleeps is night, whenever she wakes is morning. Absent sun, who's to care? They drag her down another empty hall. Commandant waits. No pliers this time. Commandant looks as tired as Red feels. She's learned exhaustion in their many sessions together, as Red has learned fear.

"Tell us," she says. "This is the last time I ask. Tomorrow, we'll take you apart and sift the pieces for what we want to know."

Red raises an eyebrow.

"Please," Commandant says, dry as steel.

Red says nothing.

She does not think about pomegranates. She does not dare hope. All they ever had was a chance. *And even if it worked, even if she woke, who's to say she'd come for you?*

You betrayed her.

Red does not think.

The guard drags her back down the long empty hall and pauses at the open door.

Red, ready to be tossed once more into her small gray world, looks back. The guard watches her with still and weighing eyes and a mouth twisted to a cruel, clever line.

"Why are you doing this?" Gruff, low. They aren't supposed to talk to prisoners.

Red's always been one for small talk. And—tomorrow's the end. "Some things matter more than winning."

The guard considers. Red knows the type: idealistic but unskilled, hoping to rise through the ranks on dependability. Yet her defection loosened this one's lips.

Blue would have been impressed.

"You broke into Garden, and out again, and you won't tell us how. So you're not on our side. Why not join them when you had the chance? Sell us out?" So earnest. Red was that way once.

"Garden doesn't deserve us. Neither does the Agency." By us she means herself and Blue, wherever she may be, if in fact she is. She means all of them, all the ghosts on all the threads dying in this sick old war. Even this guard. Red gives her this truth, at the last. Maybe it will save her life.

The guard throws her into the cell anyway.

Red hits the floor and skids. She lies still and does not look up. Something rustles behind her. The cell door shuts. All over soon. She did what she could. The guard walks away, boot thud echoing heavy, measured, slow.

When Red looks up, a small rectangle of white paper lies upon the floor.

She scrambles toward the envelope, claws it to her.

Her name. Handwriting she knows.

She remembers the guard's grip on her arm. Remembers that voice. Was it familiar?

She rips the envelope open with her thumb and reads, and by the second line, her cheeks hurt from the fierceness of her smile.

My dear Hyper Extremely Red Object—

I didn't know what you would do.

I want to explain myself—this self you've saved, this self you've infected, this self that was Möbius twisted with yours from its earliest beginning.

I planted your letter. I watched it grow. I tended it and thought of feeding it my blood, rearing a mouth in it through which to speak to you. You said not to read it. The thought of your naïveté charmed me in the same breath as the thought of betrayal burned me. It had to be one or the other: How could you think that your failure to kill me would result in anything less than your own death? How could you not see this for the test it was? How, unless you trusted in your conquest sufficiently to know I would take myself off the board for you, prompted by a clumsy show of your pain?

Either way, there was only one choice. To protect you—whatever your intentions—I had to submit to you.

It wasn't hard. Truth be told, Red—not reading your letter was harder.

When you said you wouldn't write again, when you said—that is the only letter of yours I've wanted to obliterate from myself. If I'm honest, that's part of why I took the bait. To be unmade, that last written over—to be destroyed by you was easier, truly, than living with what you proposed.

But I'm greedy, Red. I wanted the last word as well as the first.

I hope you did not take my reply too hard. I knew you might not be the first to read it. I want you to know—I died thinking that if anyone could keep me alive, it would be you. It was, I confess to you here, a smug thought: that I died by my own hand, and was raised by yours.

You remember I promised you infiltration from my very first letter—dared you to be infected by me. I couldn't know, then—I couldn't, and nor could you—how thoroughly you were already inside me, shielding me from the future. You've always been the hunger at the heart of me, Red—my teeth, my claws, my poisoned apple. Under the spreading chestnut tree, I made you and you made me.

There's still a war out there, of course. But

this is a strategy untested. What would Genghis say if we built a bridge together, Red? Suppose we reached across the burn of threads and tangles, cut through the braid's knots—suppose that we defected, not to each other's sides, but to each other? We're the best there is at what we do. Shall we do something we've never done? Shall we prick and twist and play the braid until it yields us a place downthread, bend the fork of our Shifts into a double helix around our base pair?

Shall we build a bridge between our Shifts and hold it—a space in which to be neighbours, to keep dogs, share tea?

It'll be a long, slow game. They'll hunt us fiercer than they ever hunted each other—but somehow I don't think you'll mind.

I've bought you five minutes to bust out. Instructions on overleaf, though I doubt you'll need them.

I don't give a shit who wins this war, Garden or the Agency—towards whose Shift the arc of the universe bends.

But maybe this is how we win, Red.

You and me.

This is how we win.

Acknowledgments

M: It's customary to start pieces like these with a riff on the subject of how "this book would not exist without . . . ," but I suspect this particular book would have found a way to shoulder into being in spite of adversity. Nonetheless! So many people prepared the way and shaped the final volume.

A: So many people! And while it might be in keeping with the enterprise to thank G. Lalo for producing the truly gorgeous paper that enticed two writers with more ink on their hands than time (SORRY) into a lengthy correspondence—such acknowledgments are, perhaps, beyond the scope of even this project. On to friends and family!

M: Much of our *Time War* was composed in the gazebo of an anonymous benefactor, which is a phrase I have always wanted to type. All thanks and glory to that individual. I'd say they know who they are, but they may not. Perhaps it was . . . YOU?

A: Shh, we've already said too much! But genuinely, thank you, A. B.—so many of the birds and bees around that gazebo made it into this story, and we're so grateful for the lease of them.

M: My wife, Stephanie Neely, is a constant font of strength, spirit, joy, and good humor, without which art falls silent, and she's brought me back to life on more than one occasion. She is that without which none. Love you, Steph!

A: My husband, Stu West, spent the early years of our relationship loudly proclaiming his hatred for (a) novellas and (b) cowritten works, so I can hardly begin to say how happy and grateful I am that he set those prejudices aside to love this unreservedly. His warm enthusiasm and unceasing support are a balm and a hearth. *Shukran habibi!*

M: Like any book, this one had many shepherds. Amal's parents, Leila Ghobril and Oussama El-Mohtar, generously tolerated our occupying the living room table with exclamation-point-laden notes and singing Steven Universe songs; Kelly and Laura McCullough provided vital welcome, hospitality, and throwing axes.

A: Deep, heartfelt thanks to DongWon Song and Navah Wolfe, agent and editor (respectively) both most extraordinary, for taking such a truly strange literary creature and helping us shape and refine it for you. It would not be what it is without them. Praise them with great praise! Warm thanks, too, to Felicity Maxwell, for her generous expertise on Bess of Hardwick, and to Jay Odjick, for his kind input on indigenous language-use. Any errors are of course my own.

M: It takes a village to raise a book from a vulnerable manuscript into a strong and beautiful object. Our awed and sincere thanks to our managing editor, Jeannie Ng, who kept our wiggly time-travel project on schedule; to our copyeditor Brian Luster, for a combination of eagle-eyed precision and kind forbearance; to our production manager, Elizabeth Blake-Linn, who in many invisible ways has made this book more enjoyable to hold and read; to Greg Stadnyk, who designed a jacket neither of us could have predicted but which both of us love; and to our publicist Darcy Cohan, for all her tireless work on our behalf.

A: Finally, dear reader, we dedicated this one to you, and we meant it. Books are letters in bottles, cast into the waves of time, from one person trying to save the world to another.

Keep reading. Keep writing. Keep fighting. We're all still here.

This Is How You Lose the Time War

BY AMAL EL-MOHTAR
&
MAX GLADSTONE

This reading group guide for This Is How You Lose the Time
War *includes an introduction, discussion questions, and ideas
for enhancing your book club. The suggested questions are
intended to help your reading group find new and interesting
angles and topics for your discussion. We hope that these ideas
will enrich your conversation and increase your enjoyment of
the book.*

Introduction

In the ashes of a dying world, Red finds a letter marked "Burn before reading" signed by Blue.

So begins an unlikely correspondence between two rival agents in a war that stretches through the vast reaches of time and space.

Red belongs to the Agency, a post-singularity techno-topia. Blue belongs to Garden, a single vast consciousness embedded in all organic matter. Their pasts are bloody and their futures mutually exclusive. They have nothing in common—save that they're the best, and they're alone.

Now what began as a battlefield boast grows into a dangerous game, one both Red and Blue are determined to win. Because winning's what you do in war. Isn't it?

Topics & Questions for Discussion

1. As Red and Blue are executing their respective orders, they have their first exchange. Describe the warriors introduced in these first few opening challenges. Is one more dedicated to their cause than the other?

2. Red and Blue are sworn enemies in a timeless war and while they joke about poison, "PS. The Keyboard's coated with slow-acting contact poison. You'll be dead in an hour" (page 30), they never use it. Why have they never tried to kill each other? Why do they continue to open the letters? Is it trust, or something else?

3. "Do I have you still . . . You could leave me for five years, you could return never—and I have to write the rest of this not knowing," (page 42). There are physical limitations to the way Red and Blue choose to communicate. With the most advanced technology at their fingertips, why have they chosen to leave their messages in these unique media?

4. Blue writes a lot about Atlantis in one of her early letters. Discuss why this is a myth the authors choose

to highlight and why Atlantis, of all places, recurs with the same result in every strand? Do you accept Red's explanation?

5. There are many subtle pop-culture references made as Red and Blue move through time. Which references did you pick up on? Which were your favorites?

6. Red quotes "the prophets" several times. Who do you think the prophets are for warriors out of time? Based on the quotes she recites, do you believe they are considered prophets here in the 21st century?

7. Blue speaks very little about the opposition except to say, "The thought of your disembodied network repulses me, but I look at you, Red, and see much of myself: a desire to be apart, sometimes, to understand who I am without the rest," (page 72). What do we know of Blue and Red's organizations? Would you consider them communities? What are the differences between the two?

8. The seeker appears at the end of every chapter, chasing letters and collecting evidence. Who is the seeker? What is their purpose? What is their role in this time war?

9. Discuss how Red and Blue each come to realize they are in love. What made it apparent to you? Does it happen more easily for one than the other?

10. There is little proof that the shadow Red senses is real. What proof does she offer? Sometimes even she does not completely believe her theory. What makes you believe or doubt her?

11. Red and Blue each interact with their leaders once through the book. What are the notable differences between the Commandant and Garden? Who would you rather work for?

12. Red's final letter to Blue is extremely complex. Discuss its many layers and her decision to write a letter within the poison. What would you write if you were in her position?

13. Why does Blue open Red's poison letter after Red warns her that it is a trap? Describe the tone of her dying letter. Is it a betrayal?

14. Red makes a very risky move that will have dire consequences if things don't align perfectly. How many ways could her plan go wrong? Discuss Red's mind-set before, during and at the end of this impossible mission.

Enhance Your Book Club

1. Every move in the Time War is carefully calculated and chosen for it's the far-reaching ramifications. Even chaos is purposefully created. Discuss how difficult it would be to choose the right moments to change. How does this compare to war as we know it?

2. Letters were once a primary form of communication and people had lasting relationships with their pen pals. Discuss how communication has changed and how that affects relationships. Are technological advances improvements?

3. Imagine you are an agent fighting in this Time War, dancing along the braids. What would it be like to see all the different strands? Would you like to experience all of time in the way Red and Blue do? What kind of agent would you be?